"Have you decided
you can trust me?"

His face was turned away from her, but he had been completely aware of her scrutiny.

"I think—" Jolie fought back the briefly rising flush of embarrassment "—that if you put a gold ring in your ear, you would make an excellent pirate."

He turned to study her. "From some women that might be a compliment. What a pity I'm only a poor plantation owner."

"The best things in life are free," Jolie quipped, seeking a lighter topic.

"Don't you believe it!" His laugh was cynical. "You pay dearly for everything, one way or another."

"And what price for love?" she asked.

His eyes were harsh and piercing as he glanced over her. "The most precious thing a man has . . . his freedom."

Janet DAILEY
SOMETHING EXTRA

Harlequin Books

TORONTO • NEW YORK • LONDON
AMSTERDAM • PARIS • SYDNEY • HAMBURG
STOCKHOLM • ATHENS • TOKYO • MILAN

This edition published August 1989
ISBN 0-373-83209-5

Harlequin Presents edition published August 1978
Janet Dailey Collector's edition October 1982
Romance Treasury edition April 1988

Original hardcover edition published in 1975
by Mills & Boon Limited

CHAPTER ONE

THE PINTO, a mixture of chestnut and white, reluctantly submitted to the pressure of the reins and turned away from the rich grasses of his pasture. His head bobbed rhythmically from side to side as he plodded down the rutted lane. Fifteen summers had been seen by his soft brown eyes. He no longer pranced and tossed his brown and white mane, nor tugged at the bit between his teeth. Through the years he had grown fat and lazy, saving his energy to swish away flies and tear at the long green grass so that he would have the strength to see another South Dakota winter sweep by.

The horse didn't need to look at a calendar to see the month of September preparing to make way for October. He had only to look at the trees and their green leaves that were dotted with gold and orange, or to raise his brown eyes to the blue skies and see the gathering of birds which were ready to begin the migration to the south at the first sign of cold. The waving fields of wheat next to his pasture had ripened and their grains of gold hung heavily on their slender stalks. The days were still warm, but the nights held a chill. The pinto had already begun growing his shaggy coat to ward off the cold north-west winds.

A heel dug firmly into his side, and he snorted his dislike before amiably breaking into a rocking canter. The weight on his back was light and the hands holding his reins were gentle. The pinto's dark ears pricked forward as a brightly plumed rooster pheasant took wing ahead of them. But there was not the slightest break in his stride. A hand touched the side of his neck in praise, followed by a checking of reins. The aging pinto gladly settled back into a shuffling trot and finally to his plodding walk.

The girl astride his bare back sighed deeply, letting the circled reins drop in front of her while placing her hands on her hips. Her bare legs dangled from his fat sides as she balanced herself easily on his broad back. She squinted her own soft brown eyes at the sun's glare, feeling its warmth on the skin not covered by the white halter top or the blue shorts. If she had looked for them, she would have seen all the signs of autumn that the horse did. But her gaze flitted over them all, looking but not seeing.

Her figure was adequate, not over-curvaceous nor over-slender, just somewhere in the middle. In her bare feet, she stood five feet four, an average height for an average build. Her hair was the same warm brown shade as her eyes, thick and cropped in a feathery boy-cut that allowed its thickness and natural wave to frame her oval face. Again her features were average, not possessing any startling beauty, only a pleasing wholesomeness.

When she was younger, Jolie Antoinette Smith used to moan about her lack of glamorous beauty. Her father always used to gather her in his arms in one of his giant bear hugs and in his laughing voice teased her.

"You have a pair of very nice eyes to see with; a nose to breathe and smell with; nice, generous lips to frame a mouth that talks and eats with its full set of white teeth." Then he would lift her downcast chin with his hand and study her face closely. His voice would become very serious. "And by my latest count, you have two thousand, four hundred and thirty-seven freckles, which you ought to thank the good Lord for, because he's the one who sprinkled gold dust all over your face."

She would be scowling by that time at the faint freckles that were there and not there, so light were they. Her father would then tickle the corner of her mouth, forcing her to smile.

"And he also gave you a matching set of dimples!" he ended triumphantly. Even though Jolie knew he was prejudiced in her favor, she always felt better after one of those sessions. It was only as she grew older that she realized he had been trying to make her content with the way she was, with the things she couldn't change. Yes, she had long ceased to curse the fact that she had been endowed with both freckles and dimples, too, and learned to endure the good-natured teasing that they always brought.

Even though Jolie seldom rated a second glance when she was walking down a street, the men who did become acquainted with her found that she was an excellent listener, had a ready smile, and could carry on a conversation without giggling. She was the kind of girl that got invited home to meet mother while her girl friends were invited to parties. After hearing tales of what went on at some of the parties, Jolie wasn't sure she would have liked it, but she never had the chance to find out for herself.

She was home now after a little more than three years in which she had crammed a four-year college course. She had finished her education and obtained her degree, but now what? What came next? Inside Jolie felt that surge of restlessness, that heightening sense of dissatisfaction.

She had come home and all was different while it remained the same. Home. A three hundred and sixty acre tract of land sixty miles from Yankton, South Dakota, where for the entire twenty-one years of her life, Jolie's parents had farmed. It had been a good life, and a hard life at times, the difference dictated by the weather and its effect on the crops. But it was her parents' life and not hers.

The pinto paused to munch on a tempting clump of grass until Jolie raised herself out of her indifference to lift his head away.

"If you eat any more, Scout, your sides will burst," she admonished. Dutifully the horse plodded on. "Poor old Scout," Jolie sighed, "you've changed, too, just like me. Whoever said 'You can't go home again' was right."

Her parents had lived by themselves for the last three years and had grown accustomed to it. They no longer knew how to treat Jolie. She was not a child any more, but to them she would never be quite an adult. Madelaine, her older sister by one year, was married and already had two children as well as a life completely separate from Jolie's. Change was the only constancy. And that included John Talbot.

Jolie saw his pick-up truck parked on the field turn-off of the country road. His tall, sunburned figure was standing on the edge of a wheat field, the muscles in his arms gleaming in the late morning sunlight. A stalk of wheat was between his teeth as he lifted an arm in greeting. Without any effort his long stride carried him to the edge of the field as Jolie drew level atop her pinto. His large hands encircled her waist and lifted her to the ground. There John lowered his head and with the ease of habit claimed her mouth in a kiss. Jolie responded just as naturally, liking the warmth and the closeness of his body next to hers.

"Hi." The gleam of quiet affection in his tawny gold eyes was comfortably pleasing, as was the slow smile. "It's been a long time since you've come out to visit me in the fields."

Snuggling against his shoulder, his muscular arm firmly holding her there, Jolie nodded agreement as she slipped her arm behind his back and around his waist. The pinto contentedly began grazing on the grasses near the lane, ignoring the couple walking slowly toward the lone cottonwood that stood on the edge of the wheat field.

"Dad says your wheat is ready for harvest." Jolie easily fell into the main topic of conversation in the area. It was a safe subject that steered clear of her restlessness. John plucked another stalk of wheat before sinking down on the ground beneath the shade tree. He stripped the golden grain from its head, tossing two into his mouth.

"Still a little too much moisture," he decreed. "Another day or two of sun like this and it'll be ready." He pushed the straw hat back on his light brown head and gazed out over the golden sea of grain. "It's going to be a good harvest."

"Dad's shoulder is bothering him, which means rain before tomorrow night." The blade of grass in her hand split down the middle at the nervous pressure of her fingers. She tossed it from her in disgust.

"You can tell him for me that he can hold it off for another couple of days," John smiled, and drew Jolie into his arms.

She turned her head just as he was about to kiss her and his lips instead found her cheek. But he wasn't deterred, letting his mouth wander over her neck and the lobe of her ear half-covered by her brown hair. For Jolie, there was nothing soothing in his caress and her lack of response made her feel uncomfortable. She wriggled free, plucking another blade of grass and studying it intently.

His measuring eyes were on her. Jolie could feel them trail over her face and she tried to appear undisturbed.

"What's wrong, Jo?" he asked quietly. If he was angered or hurt, there was nothing in his voice to reveal it.

"I don't know," she sighed. She glanced back at him hesitantly, letting him glimpse the melancholy expression in her eyes that silently apologized.

"You've been home a week now. No calls on any of your job applications?"

"I haven't applied anywhere." His eyebrows raised briefly at her statement, but his face remained impassive otherwise. Jolie inhaled deeply as she averted her eyes from his face. He always knew so much more of what she was thinking and she couldn't even begin to guess what was going on in his mind. "I've got my diploma and I don't even know what I want to do with it."

"Home economics graduates always make good wives," John stated.

Although there was a light, teasing air about his words, Jolie knew it was a testing statement. But how could she possibly tell John that she didn't love him, or at least not the way she wanted to love the man she would marry. What was worse, she felt so guilty for not loving him.

John Talbot was a girl's dream. Not only was he good-looking, extremely so, but he was also solid and dependable. Just looking at his tanned features, so clean-cut and handsome, made Jolie wonder if she wasn't out of her mind for not snatching up this man who had waited faithfully the last five years for her. She didn't deny that John had a magnetism that attracted her to him, but nothing happened—no bells rang, her heart didn't beat any faster—when he held her in his arms. It wouldn't be fair to marry him when she knew this.

"Did you ever wonder why I didn't give you a ring while you were at college?" the quiet baritone voice asked her.

Jolie nodded, too full of her own feelings of guilt to reply vocally.

"I knew you liked me, even loved me, but I knew you weren't in love with me." Jolie grimaced and John lifted her chin that was threatening to sink into her chest. "You were eighteen and I was twenty-four. I decided it was only fair for you to wait until you had graduated. But, to trade on an old cliché, absence hasn't made the heart grow fonder, has it?"

"I feel like the lowest beast on earth, John," Jolie whispered, "but I'm not really in love with you. I care about you more than anyone I've ever met. In my way, I do love you."

For just a moment his fingers dug into her shoulders, revealing the pain that his face didn't show. Then he had released her and was lying back against the tree trunk.

"The way you feel wouldn't satisfy either one of us for long." His smile was slow and regretful with only the barest traces of bitterness around the corners of his mouth. "So what are you going to do now? Are you going to stay around here?"

"I don't think so." There was an almost imperceptible shake of her head as Jolie replied. "I thought if I came back here to the farm it would give me a chance to put my thoughts together. After three years of being whisked along by the steady flow of classes, homework and odd jobs, I feel as if somebody has just put me ashore. I thought coming home would reorientate me but it's only made me more confused. I don't want to take just any job, but I can't keep sponging off my parents either. I've cost them enough."

"It will all work out."

"I hope it does...for both of us. John?" His gaze that had been turned unseeingly on the landscape reverted to Jolie. "Is it too much to ask that we still be friends?"

His hand reached out and ruffled her hair in a gesture reminiscent of her teenage days. "Of course," he smiled, moving agilely to his feet. She rose to stand silently beside him. "Don't be so solemn, honey," tracing the curve of her cheek with his finger. "It's not as if I'd suddenly discovered you weren't in love with me. I think I would have been more shocked if you were, and a little bit afraid that you were lying."

Jolie stood on tiptoe and planted a soft kiss on his mouth, her eyes brimming with tears she didn't have any right to shed. "Aunt Brigitte will have my scalp for letting you go."

"Don't tell me your neurotically romantic aunt is here," John laughed.

"Aunt Brigitte is a died-in-the-wool spinster. How can you possibly consider her romantic? Mother swears she would be surprised if Aunt Brigitte had ever been kissed."

"Don't you believe it. There is one woman who knows exactly what love is all about." That was a puzzling statement to Jolie and one that John was going to let her think about by herself. "Uncle Ray will be wondering where I am, so I'd better shove off."

She didn't realize at first that he was leaving until he was already several steps away from her. "John, I'm...I'm sorry," she called after him.

There was a slight stiffening of his shoulders before he turned and waved. Yet his stride quickly carried him away from her toward his car. Jolie watched him drive off before she walked over to her rotund horse still contentedly stuffing himself with grass.

The screen door slammed behind her as Jolie entered the two-story, white-framed house. She didn't feel any better or worse than before she had left that morning. Only one thing was definite and that was she would not be looking for a job anywhere near home. It wouldn't be fair to John, not that he was the type to jump off a cliff. Actually, he was the opposite, the kind who met a problem head on and conquered it.

"Hello! Who is it?" The imperious call came from the sun porch.

"It's me, Aunt Brigitte," Jolie replied, sticking her head around the door with a wave of her hand. "Where's Mother?"

"In town getting groceries." When Jolie would have gone on to her own room, her aunt motioned into the room. "Come sit with me."

The iron-gray hair was drawn into a severe bun at the back of her aunt's head. Jolie had always regarded her aunt, who was twelve years her mother's senior, as being stern and practical, but in the light of John's statement, Jolie wondered how correct her assessment was. Her features, which had always possessed the uncompromising lines of age, could quite possibly be attractive when her aunt smiled as she was doing now.

"What have you been doing since you've returned home?" Her Aunt Brigitte's questions always sounded more like commands, but then she had been a teacher for the last thirty years, Jolie mused.

On rare weekends her aunt journeyed to her only sister's, Jolie's mother, to spend two uneventful days on the farm. This was one of those rare times.

"Relaxing from the grind of all the finals, mostly and trying to figure out where and what I want to do next."

"That sounds as if it's a momentous problem." Jolie saw her aunt's lips quiver, almost breaking into a smile. Brigitte Carson glanced up, noting the troubled expression on her niece's face. "It is, isn't it?"

"Yes." Jolie sighed heavily and turned away from her aunt's searching gaze.

"Where have you been this morning?"

"Out with John."

"I'm quite sure he had an answer to your dilemma."

"Yes, he had a suggestion." Jolie's voice was soft and simultaneously firm. "I'm not in love with him, Aunt Brigitte."

It was her aunt's turn to sigh and she did. "I'm sorry to hear that. Sorry for you as well as for John. He would have been a loving husband and father. You are quite sure about how you feel?"

"What is love?" Jolie asked quietly, turning away from the window to her aunt. "I'm twenty-one years old and I don't even know what it is."

"That, my dear, is an eternal question that will be asked as long as there are people on earth." Her aunt's dark gray eyebrows raised significantly. "At least, I do know you aren't in love with John or you wouldn't ask."

"Which is a tricky way of avoiding my question." Depression turned down the corners of her mouth. "And please don't use mother's old quote—Love is many things to many people."

"The kind of love that I believe you're talking about is a rare thing where bells ring," her aunt answered her quietly. "Mostly because it's a selfless love and there are few people who can give of their feelings so freely and completely. Others search for it so hard that they never find it. There are only a lucky few who really do find it."

"Did you, Aunt Brigitte?" The withdrawn expression on her aunt's face drew the whispered question from Jolie's lips.

"Yes, once. A car accident took him away from me." A melancholy smile lifted the usually stern mouth. "And that love completely spoiled me for second best, which has made my life very lonely. The type of love you're speaking about can cost very dearly. Perhaps that's why it's so precious."

"Do you suppose I'll ever find it?"

"Not with that mopy expression on your face. Nobody would be interested in a mourner." From experience, Brigitte Carson put just enough sharpness in her teasing words to pull Jolie away from the depths of depression.

"Well, I certainly need something to do with myself in the meantime. I'm not looking forward to leaving here and still, I don't want to stay."

"Sometimes, Jolie, it's difficult to make a decision when you're surrounded by the people you know. You want their suggestions even knowing they're not helpful. The best thing for you to do would be to take off for a week or two. Go somewhere by yourself, relax, and have a good time. It's surprising how clear everything becomes afterward."

"There isn't any place I particularly care to go," Jolie shrugged.

"Oh, surely there's some place that you've always wanted to see."

A light shone for a moment in Jolie's eyes as she thought of her long-held childhood wish before she blinked it away.

"Perhaps," she admitted, "but it's quite out of the question. What little money I have saved I'll have to use to start out on my own. It wouldn't stretch to include any extravagant whims."

"It doesn't hurt to talk about it. Where would you like to go—if you could afford it?" the matronly woman persisted.

"I know this must sound awfully strange to you, but I've always wanted to go to Louisiana where my great-grandmother or whatever came from. I remember grandmother telling Madelaine and myself the stories her mother had told her about the plantation home where she lived." Jolie glanced over at her aunt, shyness creeping into her voice. "I can't help wondering if Cameron Hall is still standing."

"It is rather curious how that one lone ancestor of ours has managed to still be so much a part of our lives." Dark eyes scrutinized Jolie carefully. "You were named after her, weren't you? Jolie Antoinette. Somehow all the girls received French names down the years."

"I don't mind. Jolie is much more romantic than Jane Smith could ever be," she laughed.

"Perhaps there is a way you can make this trip." The wheels were turning almost visibly in her aunt's mind as Jolie watched her set the book from her lap and stand.

"I don't see how."

"I have a fair amount of money saved and I never have decided what I'm saving it for. I didn't get you a graduation gift because I wanted you to pick it out. It seems you have," her aunt smiled. "A trip to Louisiana and the bayou country."

"That's much too expensive!" Jolie gasped. "I couldn't possibly let you do it."

"How could you possibly stop me?"

CHAPTER TWO

EVERY ONE of Jolie's arguments was brushed off with logical rebuttals until she found herself sitting down at a desk while her aunt began planning her trip. Jolie's little Volkswagen would need to be checked thoroughly before the journey. A few dresses needed to be added to her wardrobe. Inquiries had to be made as to the accommodation in the town nearest the plantation, Cameron Hall. The amount of funds needed for gasoline, meals and lodging had to be estimated. By the time Jolie's mother arrived home from town, her itinerary had been all laid out and it was presented to her mother by Aunt Brigitte as an accomplished fact.

Looking at the total cost of the trip, Jolie moaned, "You should at least come with me, Aunt Brigitte, and get some enjoyment yourself out of this money."

"That isn't the object of the trip. The idea is for you to get off by yourself and have fun. Something you certainly couldn't do if you were dragging a spinster aunt along," her aunt had scolded with mock severity.

No amount of persuasion could alter her aunt's decision. In no time at all Jolie was swept up in the carrying out of the items on the list. Within a week her car was decreed ready for the journey, a reply had been received assuring her of available accommodation, and her suitcases were packed. When she wheeled her cranberry-colored car on the highway, Jolie was caught up in the excitement of her journey.

There was only one thing that could put a blight on her journey, Jolie decided, and that was the distinct possibility that Cameron Hall was no longer standing. The letter she had received assuring her that there was accommodation in the town had also stated that they had no knowledge of a plantation called Cameron Hall. Her aunt had been quick to point out that it had been sold shortly after the Civil War for taxes and had very likely been renamed. It was a small hope, but exceedingly logical since renaming of plantations was not an uncommon practice.

Even though she wanted to hurry, Jolie took her time during the long drive, breaking the journey into stages that would spread it over nearly four days. Leisurely she went on the scenic back roads, avoiding the modern roads that were quicker but not nearly as beautiful. Still, when the little red Volkswagen crossed the border into Louisiana, her heart beat a little faster. It was almost as if she were coming home.

It was six o'clock in the evening and Jolie was less than a hundred miles from her final destination. If it hadn't been for her strong desire to see this last portion of her journey during the daylight hours, she would have pushed on. As it was, she reluctantly turned the car into the driveway of a motel, determined that the following morning she would get an early start and allow herself ample time to view the new countryside unhurried by waning daylight.

The following morning the last leg of her journey began, out of the National Forests around Alexandria, down through Opelousas and Lafayette, until finally the turnoff for St. Martinville, the heart of the Evangeline Country, was in front of her. A road marker in the center of the town beckoned her to visit the Evangeline oak tree, immortalized in the poem by Longfellow, but Jolie steeled herself to pass it by. Almost three full weeks of sightseeing stretched ahead of her, but first she had to have a place to stay, somewhere inexpensive and still comfortable.

She parked the red Volkswagen in front of a restaurant, deciding that an inquiry of one of the local people might direct her to a place where she could rent a place of her own and save the cost of hotel rooms and meals. After ordering coffee, Jolie asked the waitress if she knew of such a place. The young girl offered her a local newspaper, but the small classified section didn't have any listings within Jolie's budget. When the waitress returned with her coffee she handed the paper back.

"I'm afraid there wasn't anything in there that was what I had in mind," she sighed. "Do you know where else I might check?"

The young dark-haired girl began to shake her head negatively before putting her hand to her mouth as if some idea had just occurred to her. She glanced toward the counter where a trio of men was sitting, then turned back to Jolie with a wide smile.

"I may know a place. Let me see," she said.

Jolie watched the waitress walk over to the group of men, tap a dark-haired man on the shoulder, and with a gesture toward Jolie, begin speaking. Seconds later he was excusing himself from the other men and accompanying the waitress to her table. His dark, blue eyes dwelt speculatively on Jolie as the young waitress introduced them.

"Miss, this is Guy LeBlanc. I think he'll be able to help you." The waitress moved away after Jolie's expression of thanks.

"I'm pleased to meet you, Miss...?" Jolie knew his wide smile was meant to charm and it did.

"Smith, Jolie Smith," she supplied, answering his smile with her own.

"Denise, the waitress, said you were looking for a boarding house," the man prompted.

"Yes, I was hoping for a place where I might have kitchen privileges. I wouldn't be staying more than a few weeks," Jolie explained, brushing back a feathery wisp of her brown hair and feeling self-conscious under his obvious scrutiny. "Do you know where I might find something like that?"

"My home," Guy LeBlanc said calmly, and laughed softly when her eyebrows raised significantly. "Where my parents also live," he added reassuringly. "In the past they've taken on boarders, although we haven't had any for some time."

"Do you suppose they could be persuaded to let me stay?" Jolie liked the man's drawling voice even while her mind tried to place the difference in his way of speaking that was not like other Southern accents she had heard.

"I'm sure, but let me take you there and you may talk to them yourself. You do understand that it will be only a large bedroom and your meals would be taken with the family." He spoke as he courteously helped Jolie slide her chair back from the table. As she reached in her bag to pay for her coffee, Guy interceded, placing change upon the table and signaling the waitress that it was for Jolie's coffee. "My pleasure," he smiled when Jolie attempted to protest.

As the pair left the restaurant, it was Jolie's turn to inspect the man walking beside her to the Volkswagen. She decided Guy LeBlanc was in his early twenties, a year or two older than herself, perhaps. He was less than six foot tall, but lean, and graceful. His hair was brown, but much darker than hers. His features echoed the slenderness of the rest of his body, with darkly arched brows, an aristocratically straight nose, and a finely drawn mouth. But his dark eyes were like burnished coals that gleamed and glittered as they reflected light. He wore dark tan trousers and a brightly printed cotton shirt that was open at the neckline. He exuded an air of confidence and ease that Jolie knew was part of his charm. She also knew that this young man was fully aware of his looks and made use of them wherever possible. A warning she herself should make note of for the future, especially if she should stay in the same house with him. His directions were very precise as he instructed Jolie along the route to his house. She had expected him to suggest that he drive her car, but he made it evident that he would rather watch her than the route they were taking.

"The white house on the corner. There's a place to park your car behind the house," he informed Jolie.

Again she puzzled over the accent in his voice that wasn't quite Southern as she followed his instructions, turning into the driveway of the large rambling house and continuing to the rear.

She had barely braked the car to a halt when Guy was out of the car and around to her side to open the door. His courtesy was a little overpowering, and Jolie wasn't too sure how to deal with it. Foolishly she reached for the handle of the back door, only to have Guy LeBlanc's hand there before her. She smiled uncomfortably when his other hand offered her entry into his home.

The room he ushered her into was some type of family room with white wicker chairs and sofas scattered about in abundance. Live plants thrived in green profusion. Some were suspended in pots from the high ceiling while other rubber-type plants were in huge tubs on the tiled floor and still others decorated white tabletops. The room had a tropical air, which wasn't unusual considering the heat and humidity that was typical of the Louisiana climate.

"If you would wait here, I'll find my parents."

Jolie nodded her compliance as he excused himself. She let her gaze stray around the room again, liking what she saw. The immense size of the house told her it was old, but it had been so well cared for that it was impossible to guess its age. Two sets of clicking shoes in the wide hallway leading to the room where Jolie waited signaled Guy LeBlanc's return with one other person.

"Here's the visitor I told you about, Mama." At Guy's side was a petite woman, standing barely five feet tall. Her hint of plumpness gave her a very maternal air, as did the escaping wisps of graying dark hair in the bun atop her head. An open, beaming smile accompanied the small hand extended to Jolie.

"My son told me you're looking for a place to stay. Miss Smith, isn't it?"

"Yes," Jolie nodded, drawn by the friendliness the older woman exhibited that had nothing to do with polite manners.

"She's much more attractive than you told me," Mrs. LeBlanc admonished her son playfully. "Is that the reason you're anxious for her to stay with us?"

Jolie couldn't stop the faint blush from filling her cheeks. She did not want this woman thinking that she was interested in her son. But at the sight of Jolie's discomfort, the small woman broke into a tinkling laugh.

"I was making a small joke," she smiled apologetically. "My son believes he's quite irresistible to the women. Be warned that he takes delight in new conquests. While you're staying with us, you'd do well to ignore two-thirds of his compliments."

"Then you do have a room that you're willing to let?" Jolie breathed in relief. Her wide smile hesitated as she realized she hadn't even inquired about the cost. It was difficult giving voice to her question because the woman was treating her as a guest and not a boarder. But the figure named was well within her budget. Jolie now had a place to stay, pleasant surroundings and with pleasant people.

"Tell me, Miss Smith," Guy inserted himself into the conversation quietly, "why did you choose St. Martinville as the place to spend your vacation? Why not the more resplendent and exciting New Orleans?"

"Guy!" Mrs. LeBlanc reprimanded her son sharply. "We have much to offer a visitor, and only minutes away. Our own Acadian House Museum and Craft Shop and the Acadian Heritage Museum in Loreauville. The magnificent Shadows on the Teche ante-bellum home is in New Iberia. And what about Avery Island and its Bird City and Jungle Gardens? Don't listen to him," she instructed Jolie. "There's plenty here for you to do. If you wish to visit New Orleans, it's only a short journey away."

"I know I'm going to enjoy myself here," Jolie agreed as she wondered why she was hesitating about confiding the main reason for her journey—to find the plantation home of her great-grandmother. "There was another reason I came here particularly." She glanced from mother to son. "An ancestor of mine once lived on a plantation near here. My namesake, actually. Jolie Antoinette Cameron. The plantation was Cameron Hall. Perhaps you've heard of it?"

She held her breath as the two paused before replying.

Guy LeBlanc shrugged his shoulders, accompanying it with a negative shake of his head and a small smile. But his mother didn't give up so quickly.

"Do you know where it is from here?" she asked.

"I only know it was ten or fifteen miles from St. Martinville."

"That's not much," the woman added. Her soft voice conveyed a sadness that Jolie didn't want to feel. "The years didn't treat many of our old homes kindly. What old age, termites and fire didn't destroy fell before the winds of the hurricanes and the creeping hand of progress."

"You don't think there's much chance that the plantation is still standing?" Jolie inhaled deeply. The lifting of her chin indicated that she wasn't giving up without even trying.

''There are a few old derelicts standing about the countryside,'' Guy told her. His perception told him that success with Jolie was linked with her desire to find the mansion.

''What did you say the name was again?'' Mrs. LeBlanc asked, a finger resting on the corner of her mouth.

''Cameron Hall.''

''You don't suppose Etienne's old house—'' She turned toward her son, then shook her head, ''But no, that was called the Temple, wasn't it? I confused the name of the plantation with his own. Still, he is knowledgeable about such things. We'll ask him if he knows of your place. Now we must make you comfortable in our home. Guy, bring her luggage in while I show Miss Smith—may I call you Jolie?—to her room.''

Jolie passed the car keys to Guy, adding her insistence that they call her Jolie. Only when she began following Mrs. LeBlanc down the wide hallway to the staircase leading upstairs did it dawn on Jolie what the unusual accent was in the LeBlancs' manner of speaking. It was so obvious, she wondered why she hadn't realized it earlier. It was French.

''Have you and your family lived here long?'' she asked, her hand holding the carved wooden balustrade.

"In St. Martinville? All our lives, both my husband Emile and myself," Mrs. LeBlanc replied quickly. "We bought this house a few years after we were married. My Emile was handy with his hands and even though the house was in terrible shape, he worked and fixed it until it is as you see it today."

"It's very beautiful," Jolie agreed. "Did your family emigrate from France?"

"You don't know the history of Louisiana?" Mrs. LeBlanc stopped before reaching the top of the stairs, turning to enforce an answer to her gently worded question.

"Just what most people know and what little that was included in the history books," Jolie flushed, wishing suddenly that she had done some studying before making the journey down here.

"Then you haven't heard the story of the Acadian people?" Jolie shook her head from side to side that she hadn't. "But you have heard of the Cajuns, haven't you?" Mrs. LeBlanc smiled as Jolie nodded yes.

"Acadians were emigrants from France to Canada where they settled in Nova Scotia. When England claimed the territory of Canada, she feared the large settlement of French people, so she gave them a choice of either returning to France or settling in the American colonies. Over half chose the colonies where they were scattered throughout. Many families and lovers were separated during the journey, some of them searching for years before they found those they had lost. Almost ten years later these Acadians migrated to Louisiana. The fertile land along the Mississippi River had already been grabbed up by the large plantation owners, so the Acadians settled along the bayous. After the United States purchased the Louisiana territory from France, Americans came into their new land and met these Acadian peoples. Somehow they corrupted the name Acadian to 'Cajun.' So you see Acadians and Cajuns are one in the same. Our family's ancestry goes back to these Acadian settlers. So we are really French-Canadian Americans.''

Mrs. LeBlanc clicked her tongue. ''I didn't mean to recite a history lesson,'' she apologized. ''I don't want you to be bored before you've even seen your room. Please follow me.''

''I assure you I wasn't in the least bored. I have a great deal to learn, I can see that,'' Jolie smiled, her eyes widening in emphasis. ''What little you told me just now convinces me that I'm going to find it fascinating.''

''I hope you do.'' The woman led the way down a hallway almost as wide as the one downstairs. ''The bathroom is at the end of this hall, and here's your room.'' After opening a door, she stepped back, allowing Jolie to enter the room first. "Do you like it?"

"It's so big!"

Jolie didn't know how she could begin to explain that she would have been satisfied with a room half the size. Instead she was standing in a large, high-ceilinged room with two large windows that were nearly floor to ceiling. One corner of the room near the windows held a small desk and a chair along with a cushioned armchair and floor lamp. A single bed and large maple dresser were the other pieces of furniture in the room. Throw rugs the color of a pale blue sky were scattered about the polished wood floors, bringing out the pastel colors in the print material in the bedspread and the cushioned armchair. The whole effect was spacious cosiness.

"This was my eldest daughter's room before she was married," Mrs. LeBlanc explained. "It's large enough to give you privacy without making you feel cramped."

"How many children do you have?" Jolie asked as her landlady revealed the concealed door to the closet, delighting Jolie even more.

"Five. Two of my older girls are married. Claudine is still living with us part of the year. My youngest daughter, Michelle, teaches school here. And of course, our baby of the family, Guy."

"The little boy who's abominably spoiled," Guy laughed, poking his head around the door. "Is it safe to come in? I don't want to interrupt if you were about to begin praising me to Miss Jolie Smith."

"At least he admits he's spoiled," Mrs. LeBlanc winked to Jolie. Her dainty hand waved her son into the room. "Bring her suitcases in, Guy. Then I'm sure you have some work to do, so our new guest will have time to settle in."

He placed her suitcases near the bed, his dark eyes dwelling on her with an intentness Jolie knew was supposed to send her heart pounding, but it maintained its steady pace. His exaggerated reluctance to leave was revealed by his long sigh as he promised to see her later. Once Guy had left the room Mrs. LeBlanc turned to Jolie and laughed.

"My son, the lover. I'll leave you to unpack. We'll be having a cold lunch around one o'clock. The dining room is the second door on the right from the stairway."

CHAPTER THREE

"DON'T YOU work somewhere, Guy?" Jolie half asked and half demanded.

"Would it be so great a crime if I didn't?" he mocked, firmly tucking her hand under his arm as they strolled down the sidewalk.

"It would be a waste," she returned brightly.

"And it would disappoint you that I haven't a profession?"

"Why should it disappoint me?"

"Because, from what you've told me, I know that you come from a hard-working family, so therefore a man who lazes about would be considered disreputable. Since I don't want you to think unkind thoughts about me, I'll confess that I'm an accountant with my own very small business."

Jolie knew her astonishment registered in her face, but she couldn't hide it. Guy LeBlanc was not her idea of an accountant, not with his suavity and good looks. A salesman would have been a more logical profession for him.

"Your expression of disbelief wounds my pride." His dark eyes looked dutifully hurt.

"It's really very logical. I am self-employed and have no one to answer to for the hours I keep or don't keep but myself. I derive an ample income with little time expended. There are times when I have much to do, but even more times when I have very little to do. And during the times I have very little to do, I can escort attractive young women around town and show them our points of interest. Very convenient, wouldn't you say?"

"I think you're trying to paint yourself as much more of a rogue than you really are." Jolie's knowing smile carved two very deep dimples in her cheeks.

"Women love rogues. They have a touch of the forbidden fruit about them. Plus women are born reformers. They enjoy trying to make an honest man out of me, and if I should stray—" Guy winked. "It is, after all, only my nature."

"And there's safety in numbers," Jolie agreed.

"For the time being." He let their pace slacken. "I have a hunch you could be my undoing."

"Me?" Jolie laughed incredulously. "Why?"

"Because you could make a man want to change." Despite his smile, there was gravity in his gaze.

"After twenty-one years of looking at my reflection in a mirror, I know I don't have the beauty to turn a man's head," Jolie smiled, "so your flattery won't get you anywhere with me, Guy LeBlanc."

"No, I'm speaking the truth. If you were in a room with the most beautiful women in the world, yours is the face a man would remember. It would come back to haunt him with its serene animation. A contradiction, I admit, but it's the only way of describing that combination of pale boyish freckles, dimples and soft brown eyes. A man thinks serious thoughts when he looks at you," Guy declared firmly.

"The girl you take home to mother," Jolie nodded, pleased by his sincere words, but, like all women, wishing she were the type that sent a man's heart racing and his head spinning with thoughts of anything but "mother"!

"A girl he would be extraordinarily proud to take home to mother," Guy corrected quietly.

"I think you suffer from a lack of competition." The conversation had become more personal than Jolie wanted. And it called for a change of subject.

"Oh, I have competition, very formidable competition." The dark-haired man at her side inhaled deeply.

"I must meet him so I can compare notes," Jolie teased. "Who is he?"

"No, no, you don't get his name from me," Guy laughed. "Besides, he's older and too experienced for you. You're much safer with me."

"Now, why would you admit that?"

"I'm thinking of my sister who has him all marked out as her personal property, for one thing. And secondly I don't think he'd let your air of innocence deter him. So be warned!" His dark brows raised as he emphasized his air of intrigue.

Jolie merely laughed, the throaty sound rolling out from deep within her. "How far is it now to the oak tree?"

"Just around the corner. How familiar are you with Longfellow's poem, *Evangeline*?" Guy asked.

"Only the gist of it. I remember Evangeline was separated from her fiancé, Gabriel, and that she searched until she found him dying in a hospital."

"Have you heard the story upon which the poem was based?" When Jolie said no, that she hadn't, Guy continued. "An orphan girl named Emmeline Labiche was taken in by an Acadian family and raised in their home in Nova Scotia. When she was sixteen she was to marry Louis Arceneaux from the same village. This was during the time when the English were transporting the Acadian families out of Canada. Louis attempted to resist the deportation, was injured and carried away by the English and was thus separated from Emmeline when she was taken to another ship. Emmeline and her foster family ended up in Maryland, but she had no idea where Louis was. After several years they heard of the settlement of some Acadians in Louisiana and Emmeline accompanied her family here. When she stepped off the boat, her sadness vanished, because under a large oak tree she saw the man for whom she had pined all those long years. There was no happy reunion, however, because Louis had become promised to another woman. The story goes that after that meeting she still talked of him as if he were dead or in some far-off land until she died.''

His step slowed and finally ceased. ''This is said to be the oak tree where Emmeline found and lost again her fiancé, Louis.''

Jolie stared at the spreading oak tree before them, its enormity dwarfing the tiny park that contained it. Beyond were the gleaming waters of a quiet stream, a scene of peaceful melancholy in almost the center of town. Here was the *Evangeline* oak tree.

''I think it's rather ironic that the building that houses the Acadian House Museum was the one that Louis Arceneaux and his new wife lived in,'' Guy said as Jolie continued gazing at the tree with its large girth and trunk-size limbs. ''We have a monument to each of them.''

"The river on the other side of the tree, that's the one that Emmeline's boat came on?" She slowly made her way across the green grass to the water in question.

"Correction." Guy followed her. "That's a bayou, more specifically Bayou Teche."

"It looks just like a small river to me," Jolie turned her puzzled brown eyes to the slim man walking beside her. "I was always under the impression that a bayou was a swamp or, at least, a swampy area."

"One of the first Frenchmen that saw one called it 'sleeping water,' because it has no discernible current," Guy explained patiently. "The water does flow, but it may change direction and flow one way and for no apparent reason reverse its flow."

"Just drifting along in leisurely Gallic fashion," she smiled. "'Teche' is French, right? What does it mean?"

"Not really. It's a corruption of an Indian word for 'Snake' which the French softened to fit their accent."

Sighing deeply, Jolie turned to Guy. "I certainly have a lot to learn."

"Good."

"Why?" She stared at him with amused astonishment.

"If you have a lot to learn, we may be able to persuade you to stay longer." He turned his sexiest smile on her. "And I'd like that very much."

"Has anybody ever told you that you come on too strong?" Her teasing question caught Guy off guard, but only for a moment.

"Only girls who haven't been the object of my attention." This time he made fun of himself.

"Such conceit!" Jolie laughed as Guy could no longer keep a straight face either.

A car pulled up to the curb near the miniature park and honked its horn, drawing both Guy and Jolie's attention. A dark-haired girl waved to them from the driver's seat.

"Now do you believe how popular I am?" His shoulders lifted in a Gallic gesture in which he mockingly resigned himself to the Fates.

"Do you want a ride home?" the girl called out.

Guy turned to Jolie. "It's a long walk. Would you rather ride?"

"I wouldn't want to cramp your style," Jolie teased impishly. "And I wouldn't want to be the object of one of your fan's jealousy."

"I think I can handle two women at the same time. I didn't tell you I was very adept at juggling," he returned with the same amount of jest.

"Okay, we'll ride home. I'm dying to see you in action," she laughed, accepting his guiding arm as he led her to the car.

"You sure took your time making up your mind," the girl stated as Guy helped Jolie into the front seat, squeezing her in the middle as he joined her. "Didn't you realize that was a 'no parking' zone?"

"We were debating whether we wanted to walk back," Guy replied. Jolie flashed him a gleaming smile at the reproving words from their driver. His finesse hadn't impressed this girl very much.

"In this heat! You've got to be kidding! Why, it would sap you of all your energy." The dark-haired girl quickly changed gears and pulled into the main thoroughfare.

Turning her gaze very briefly from the road ahead, the girl cast a quick, assessing glance over Jolie who did the same. Their driver was fairly attractive with brown hair darker than Jolie's yet not as black as Guy's. Its medium length with a side parting was flipped up at the ends to add fullness to the thin face. A pair of gold-rimmed glasses gave her dark eyes a luminous quality that added something to their childlike roundness.

"Since Guy isn't anxious to introduce us, we might as well do it ourselves," the girl flashed a quick smile to Jolie. "I'm his sister, Michelle."

"My name is Jolie Smith," Jolie replied, casting a sideways glance at Guy's bland expression. "I've rented a room from your parents for a few weeks."

"On vacation? Or are you planning to stay?"

"Vacation."

"And my dearest brother was showing you the sights." Michelle gave Guy a knowing look which he returned with an amazingly innocent expression. She added with a chuckle, "How do you always manage to find the attractive ones?"

"I'm a magnet. They find me," he grinned. "How were the little brats today?"

"Don't ask!" Michelle raised her eyes heavenward. A mockingly sad look swept over her face as she glanced at Jolie. "I teach here. Would you believe somebody let the chameleon out of the terrarium today. And it amazingly always managed to pop up on some girl's desk. I've heard enough shrieking today to last a lifetime. I think the little creature was delighted to be returned to his glass world."

"Don't let her grumbling fool you," Guy confided to Jolie. "She likes it as much as boys like girls."

"You have a one-track mind." Jolie shook her head sadly.

"You've noticed that, too," Michelle agreed.

"He led me to believe you were one of his numerous conquests."

"Okay, you two, stop ganging up on a poor defenseless male," Guy protested vigorously. "How is Jolie ever going to appreciate me if you treat me so disrespectfully?"

"The fragile male ego," Michelle whispered, drawing a laugh from Jolie.

"Didn't mother teach you that whispering is rude?" Guy asked in false anger. "Whatever she told you, Jolie, you just ignore it."

"Someone needs to forewarn her about our 'Southern gentlemen,'" his sister laughed.

Further conversation was halted by their arrival at the LeBlanc home. When Guy would have resumed his baiting with his sister, his mother appeared in the archway of the back door to welcome them. It was an unusual experience for Jolie. She suddenly discovered that she didn't feel the least bit strange or uncomfortable among these people she had only met today. They had opened their hearts as well as their arms, extending that precious gift of friendship.

"Well, what do you think of my sister?" Guy asked as Michelle succumbed to her mother's offer of assistance in carrying her papers into the house.

"She's marvelous," Jolie smiled. "I don't know why you warned me about her."

"Warn you? When did I do that?" His gaze was puzzled as he held the door for her.

"You said she had your competition all staked out as her property," Jolie reminded him.

"Competition? Who are you talking about?" Michelle asked after overhearing Jolie's reply.

"I wasn't referring to Michelle." Guy ignored his sister. "I was talking about Claudine."

"Ahhh!" Michelle's dark eyes rolled widely towards Jolie. "Now I know what you were talking about. I'm surprised you were brave enough to mention Steve to Jolie."

"He didn't ... at least, not by name." A wicked gleam lighted her eyes as she surveyed the disgruntled Guy. "So his name is Steve. I must remember that."

"I'm glad Claudine isn't here. She'd claw your eyes out for such a statement, even if you are only joking." The slight seriousness behind his words told Jolie that what he said was true.

"Since Guy refused to tell me about him you're going to have to, Michelle." She couldn't help being intrigued by this unknown Romeo.

"Fire burns, and if you get too near Steve, you get scorched," Michelle replied cryptically. "Give me my safe, solid and comfortable Gene any day."

Guy pounced on her slight change of subject eagerly. "Can you believe she's fallen for the

Ancient History teacher? Socrates and Eurip-
ides are her rivals.''

He dodged a playful, flying fist directed at
him before the sibling rivalry was set aside by
the arrival of their mother in the family room.
She carried a tray of glasses and a pitcher of
lemonade. No one had to be persuaded to indulge in the refreshment.

''I heard you talking about Claudine. I had a
letter from her today,'' Mrs. LeBlanc inserted
during a lull in the conversation. ''She's coming home this weekend.''

''For how long?'' Guy's grim expression revealed more thoroughly than his words his dis-
pleasure at the news.

''I imagine until the holidays,'' his mother
answered.

''She must have an excellent job to be able to
take off from work that amount of time,'' Jolie
commented when the silence started to stretch
awkwardly.

''My daughter's an artist, a painter,'' Mrs.
LeBlanc explained. ''She exhibits in New Orleans during the summer and again during the
winter holidays and Mardi Gras. The rest of the
year she spends here at home painting new can-
vases so that she always has an adequate sup-
ply.''

''What an exciting profession,'' said Jolie,
glancing around at Michelle and Guy, expect-

ing them to show the pride that their mother displayed. "She must be fairly successful."

"Oh, she is," the older woman nodded quickly.

"Practically all of the paintings you see here in the house were done by Claudine."

The two paintings that adorned the walls in her own room sprang quickly to Jolie's mind. They were a pair of matching yet different floral bouquets of white daisies, starburst flowers and baby's breath against a background of palest blue-gray, arranged in identical vases of Chinese design, predominantly colored in bright blue. If those were Claudine's work, then Jolie decided she was probably a very successful artist. When questioned, Mrs. LeBlanc confirmed that they were her daughter's paintings. She would have continued extolling Claudine's accomplishments, but she was interrupted by the arrival of her husband.

Emile LeBlanc was a man of small stature, standing only five feet six inches in height with a youthfully slender build. His hair had quite likely been as dark as Guy's, but now the sides were silvery white with graying steaks through the rest of his abundant mane. After greeting his family, placing an affectionate kiss on his wife's cheek, he turned to Jolie with an inquisitive smile. She was in no doubt where Guy inherited his charm.

"Who is this lovely young lady gracing our room, Josephine?"

Mrs. LeBlanc immediately explained the circumstances surrounding Jolie's presence as she made the introduction. Mr. LeBlanc's welcome was as generous as the rest of his family and almost as teasingly affectionate as Guy's.

"Jolie Antoinette are very French names to be attached to such a common one as Smith," he commented. Jolie went over again her reason for coming to St. Martinville: to try to locate the plantation her namesake once lived in as well as to tour the local sites.

Emile LeBlanc drew the same blank as did his wife and son at the mention of Cameron Hall, but he was immediately enthusiastic about the sights to be seen in the area.

"We must draw you an itinerary so that you don't miss anything during your stay with us," he decreed, looking to his son and daughter to assist with the task.

"There's time enough for that later, Papa," Mrs. LeBlanc inserted firmly. "I'm sure Jolie would much rather finish her drink, and take a shower before dinner. She can't possibly be adjusted to our humidity or rested from her long journey. Any planning can be done this evening. We mustn't force our plans on to her anyway."

"True, true," he nodded, turning to Jolie with a quick apology.

"I'm completely unfamiliar with this area, Mr. LeBlanc, and I certainly would appreciate any suggestions you would like to make," she assured him.

"Still, my wife is right. These discussions should wait until after our evening meal." His arm curled around the older woman. "What are we having tonight? Have you planned a special treat for our new guest?"

"Not this night. Let her become accustomed to our climate, then our cuisine."

Jolie tried to express the feeling of guilt possessing her that she was disrupting their life which was one thing she didn't want to do. But her protests fell on deaf ears as Mrs. LeBlanc vehemently denied that Jolie was causing her the least bit of inconvenience. She too much enjoyed the warmth of this family circle to do anything but give in.

CHAPTER FOUR

IT WAS late the following morning before Mrs. LeBlanc was satisfied that Jolie had sufficient food, drink, brochures and directions to enable her to set out on an all-day sightseeing expedition. But at last she was safely behind the wheel of her cranberry Volkswagen and turning it out of the drive.

Despite all the places listed for her to see, Jolie didn't really have any idea where she was going. The day promised to be oppressively warm, so she wasn't particularly interested in walking through museums. Besides, she didn't think her jade green cotton knit slacks with the matching midriff-length top with its peasant-style neckline and sleeves were what should be worn to such places, even if it was acceptable.

Finally she decided to journey along the back roads surrounding St. Martinville and discover what the country was like from other than a major highway. Later, when the coolness of the coming night arrived, she could stop at the Longfellow-Evangeline State Park.

St. Martinville was quickly left behind as Jolie chose a secondary highway leading from the city on the east. Traffic was non-existent and she was able to let the little car toodle along at any pace she chose, slowing down when something caught her eye as it often did, or speeding up so the self-generated wind would blow over her face.

Fields of sugar cane dominated the landscape. Some towered over her car while other younger fields barely reached her window. Scattered along both sides of the road were houses, some no different in appearance than those of her home state. Yet occasionally Jolie caught a glimpse of a large two-story home setting back from the road with finely groomed lawns and rows of oak trees leading back to it. Then she would slow down, striving to see a sign that might identify it as Cameron Hall. But she was always disappointed.

Yielding to the sense of adventure that had overtaken her, Jolie turned off the paved road onto a combination dirt and white rock. At least, she thought it was white rock, only to discover that it wasn't rock at all, but sea shells. More cane fields rose on each side of the car until Jolie felt she was being swallowed up by the grasslike crop. Only the distant branches of trees ahead promised a respite from the unbroken scenery of cane.

Jolie was accustomed to associating trees with dwellings. So when the sugar fields gave way to the trees, she was surprised and delighted to have her first look at the stagnant backwater of a marsh. Dismal cypress trees rose gloomily out of their watery habitat. The trees appeared all the more melancholy because of the Spanish moss draped among their branches. Water hyacinths fought with algae for control of the surface, their clogging green leaves giving way only to the tiny islands of marsh grass and the spiky leaves of the palmetto.

The Volkswagen's pace was slowed to that of a turtle as Jolie tried to catch a glimpse of the wildlife of the marsh. Except for an occasional flutter of wings, she saw none, which was a letdown since she would have loved to see an alligator in the wild. Jolie reconciled herself to the fact that this swamp was very small, really only a backwash, and quite probably too near human civilization to boast an alligator.

A few more feet and the swamp gave way to pasture land. The sight of cattle munching on the thick grasses seemed unnatural to Jolie, especially when they appeared to be crossbred with Brahman. Here were animals that should be in the wild and woolly section of the western United States; instead they were in Louisiana.

The road made a gentle curve around the pasture and Jolie discovered with some surprise that now on the opposite side of the road was a lazy, meandering thread of water that she immediately realized was a bayou. Sunlight shimmered across its mirrorlike surface, letting its becalmed state reflect the serenity of a peaceful scene. A crane was feeding along the rushes on the opposite bank where an oak tree's branches dipped low over the water. The ends of the moss draped over its branches were floating in the water.

Jolie decided it was an idyllic place to eat the picnic Mrs. LeBlanc had packed for her. Obligingly there was a turn-off to a field gate on the opposite side of the road where she could park her car without obstructing traffic. She didn't hesitate using it.

With the picnic basket and rug on one arm and her purse and the Thermos on the other, Jolie crossed the road toward the bayou. Somehow she managed to jump the water-filled ditch that separated the road from the banks of the bayou without dropping anything or slipping in herself.

But even if she had, Jolie thought, it would have been worth it to have a first hand look at this peaceful, tranquilizing scene. The heavy stillness from the heat of the day hung over everything. Any movement was languid and slow like the stalking crane who in slow motion raised and lowered his stilt-like legs. The calls of the birds were muted, as if conserving energy. There wasn't even the small sound of water lapping against the bank.

Beads of perspiration collected on her forehead where it matted the wispy fringes of her hair and on her upper lip so that the salty taste was on her lips. Without the benefit of the slight breeze that had been generated by her car's movement, her clothes felt sticky, clinging to her skin and increasing the discomfort of the tropical weather.

Kneeling on the short grass, she spread out the rug and arranged the other items beside it. Inside the picnic basket, Mrs. LeBlanc had placed a washcloth already moistened in a plastic bag. Jolie used its cooling dampness to wipe the perspiration from her face. The relief was immediate as the new moisture evaporated from her skin. She gazed about her, slowly continuing the wiping, but now concentrating on her neck and shoulders. The elastic in the scooped neckline of her peasant midriff blouse had been irritating, so she slipped the short sleeves down until the neckline was a straight line from upper arm to upper arm. Tilting her head back, she squeezed the cloth until droplets of water trickled over her shoulders, some finding their way to the cleavage of her breasts.

Her slow wandering gaze traveled from the view of the opposite bank to cover the surroundings nearest her. Fifteen feet to her left was another oak tree, still just a youngster compared to other giants of the same species she had seen. As her gaze trailed down the upper branches to the trunk and the ground below, her hand ceased its cooling motion with the washcloth as Jolie stared at the man reclining beneath the tree. An embarrassing rush of color warmed her cheeks, for the man was boldly and openly studying her.

Quickly her hands pulled her sleeves to their former positions, returning the midriff blouse to its more modest neckline. At her acknowledgment of his presence, the man rolled gracefully to his feet, moving out of the shade of the tree to within several paces of her. Unwillingly, Jolie moved backward.

"It seems a pity to cover such attractive shoulders." His drawling voice had a seductive softness that did little to slow the pace of her heart already beating rapidly with fear.

Jolie's hands moved out to collect her various items. "I'm . . . I'm sorry," she stammered. "I didn't realize anyone was here. I'll . . . I'll find another pl . . . place."

"There's no need," he replied. "I'm quite willing to share this view of the bayou."

Something in his cultured voice seemed to demand that Jolie raise her eyes to him. She found herself staring into the darkest pair of blue eyes that she had ever seen. They gleamed mischievously at her from the shadows of dark, curling eyelashes. In contrast, his brows and hair were black, as black as a shimmering raven's wing. His skin had tanned to a shade of teak brown and there was not the slightest variance in the shade from his legs, bared by the levi cut-offs he wore, to his arms. The man was tall, but not overpoweringly so, standing perhaps just over six feet. His physique was trim, yet not slender, displaying a sinewy strength in his arms without bulging muscles, with fine wide shoulders, a flat stomach and narrow hips.

Her assessment of his physical attributes was made with the lightning speed of the mind, but it didn't go unnoticed by the stranger. He smiled, showing a flash of pearl-white teeth, and Jolie couldn't avoid observing the grooves that deepened on either side of his mouth.

"I promise I won't pounce on you." The hint of amusement that lurked behind his words sent another tide of pink into her cheeks.

"It never occurred to me that you would," Jolie lied, knowing full well it was the first thought that entered her mind.

"It should have, because the thought certainly crossed my mind." His eyes narrowed wickedly as they traveled over her kneeling form.

Jolie longed to take a deep breath, but knew it would betray her discomfort. Instead she continued gathering her gear together.

"I don't want to intrude on your privacy," she explained when she finally had the courage to speak again.

"You're not." The man walked over to his place beneath the tree and resumed his reclining position. "Your picnic isn't going to disturb my fishing, so you might as well say."

Her gaze flicked over to the rod and reel propped up by a stick near the bank's edge. Amidst the taller grass near the edge, she spied a red tackle box.

"This is hardly the time of day to fish. It's too hot." Her natural candor blurted her opinion out before Jolie had a chance to think.

"Sounds like you've done some fishing," he drawled, only mild interest evident in his voice.

"Some," Jolie agreed, ceasing her movements that would hasten her leaving.

"I have a theory about fishing at this time of the day," turning his smile once again on her. "Want to hear it?"

"What is it?" She settled back on to the wine-colored rug, her curiosity aroused in spite of her common sense.

"I believe that the big fish are the intelligent ones that have discovered all the tricks a fisherman uses to lure them to the bait. That means they've probably also figured out that fishermen always go fishing when it's normal feeding time for fish. Therefore the big fish eat during the times that fishermen aren't about. Then he retreats to the bottom, his stomach full, when the fishermen do come.''

"Has your theory proved out?" A smile widened her mouth, carving the ever-present dimples in her cheeks.

"No," he admitted with a rueful gleam. "But my worms are getting some exercise."

Laughter rolled freely out of her throat at his preposterous assertion, but her laughter was silenced when his rod bent nearly double. With breathless disbelief Jolie watched him grab the pole, give it a quick jerk, then pull the line sharply out of the water well up onto the bank. She had a fleeting glimpse of an object on the end of the line before it disappeared from view in the grass. He reached down to pick it up as she scrambled over for a closer look.

"It's a crawdaddy!" she hooted.

"Down here, we call them crawfish," he corrected, eluding its pincers as he picked it up and placed it in a small pail.

"That's a crawfish?" Jolie stared at it, wonder creeping into her voice that this common creature, a larger version, was the famed crawfish.

"Have you heard the story of the Cajun people and their migration here from Canada?" he
asked.

"Yes." She glanced up at him curiously,
wondering what that had to do with a crawfish.

"Have you heard the legend of the crawfish?"

"No," Jolie replied, accompanying the shake
of her head with a slight sound of amusement.

"When the Acadians, or Cajuns, were forced
to leave Canada, their close friend, the lobster,
who lived in the icy waters around Nova Scotia, hated to see them leave. Naturally there was
no room for the lobster to journey with them on
the ships taking the Acadians away, so the lobster had to follow behind. They swam all the
way down the Atlantic coast, into the Gulf of
Mexico, finally arriving in the bayous of Louisiana where the Acadians had made their new
home. But the trip had made its mark. Fatigue
reduced the lobsters to a quarter of their previous size." His deep blue eyes glanced toward
her, an eyebrow arching as if saying she could
believe it or not. "So goes the legend of the
crawfish."

"Well, whether it's true or a lot of sentimental nonsense, I like it," she sighed, a hint of
satisfaction in the sound.

"Has my children's tale eased your nervousness enough to persuade you to go ahead and

have your picnic here?'' The impish twinkle was back in his gaze.

''Yes.'' A breathlessness crept into her voice as he held her gaze, but Jolie successfully rid herself of it. ''There's plenty to eat. Would you like to join me?''

''I thought you'd never ask,'' he teased.

''I didn't want to distract you from proving your theory. I'd hate to think of myself as the cause for the big fish to slip away,'' she returned, laughing as she led the way back to where her picnic basket sat. ''Of course, if the big fish are as smart as you think, they probably heard what you said and are wise to your game.''

She liked the hearty sound of his laughter as he joined in with her. But then there were quite a lot of things about this stranger that appealed to her besides his quite devastating good looks, and not the least was his sense of humor. Yet his air of self-assurance, revealed in the clever way he had set about putting her at ease, told Jolie that she was dealing with someone out of her league in experience. She couldn't allow his roguish charm to go to her head.

Even with her own warning ringing in her ears, she couldn't resist returning his smile as he settled on the rug beside her. She placed the bag of potato chips between them before reaching into the basket to withdraw the rest of the fare.

Mounds of sliced roast beef had been sand-
wiched between a loaf of French bread that had
been divided in half to provide two portions.
Jolie handed one to him and set the other aside
for herself.

"You can have your choice of apples or
oranges or both," she offered. "There's two of
each in here."

"This is plenty, thanks."

A mutual silence drifted over them as they
ate, letting the savory food predominate. Jolie
was forced to admit she was enjoying it. She was
under no pretense to keep a witty conversation
going, nor was there any personal delving into
her life. For the first time she felt free to be herself and not live up to any expectations belong-
ing to someone else, such as her parents or
John.

As she reached for the Thermos of lemon-
limeade, Jolie realized there was only one cup.
Then she shrugged inwardly that it really didn't
matter. She filled the cup and passed it to him
with a laughing apology that they would have to
share the cup as well as the food.

"Are you an Acadian?" Jolie asked when he
had passed the cup back to her after drinking his
fill.

"Only by way of believing in their philosophy."

"Which is?"

"...It is better to live than exist, better to sing than curse, better to make love than war. Or more simply, an Acadian likes strong coffee, laughter, conversation, singing, dancing, rich foods and most of all women."

"You left out Acadian women. Is that what they like too?" Jolie teased.

"They would probably include babies and gossip and their husbands."

"That's unfair!" she protested. "You just said that Acadian men like women, but the Acadian women are restricted to liking their husbands."

"You have to consider that the Acadians have certain Gallic tendencies that allow them to appreciate the beauty of every woman regardless of their marital status." Jolie could tell that he was deliberately being provocative, but still it irritated, even if only slightly.

"Always the great lovers, huh?" she said scornfully.

"Don't you find it exciting and romantic for men to pay you compliments?" He took the orange that was in her hand and began peeling it. "Frenchmen know that women take on an added glow when they're flattered. For instance, he might tell you that your hair is shiny and thick and he wonders what it would be like to tangle his fingers in its feathery curls. Or that your freckles keep you perpetually young with memories of sun-drenched summer days? And those soft brown eyes remind him of a wary doe wondering if she should dare enter a strange meadow?" Blue eyes dwelt thoughtfully on each feature he mentioned. "And the soft, rounding curve of your lips promises a yielding sweetness."

His gaze locked on hers, refusing to let her turn away. Jolie realized she was experiencing the full potency of his magnetism. The peeled orange was in his hand and he tore off a section, carrying it to her lips. Her mouth opened automatically to accept it, leaving Jolie with the feeling that she was eating the forbidden fruit.

From somewhere she drew out the sound of amused laughter, forcing herself to break away from his gaze, and wondering why she felt like crying.

"I'm glad that Frenchman isn't around," she said, trying for lightness as she busied her hands gathering up the remnants of their meal. "I would have felt guilty shrugging off his patronizing compliments."

"Is that what they seemed to you?"

"Let's just say that his poetic embellishments were a little too...poetic." An unnatural smile curved her mouth. "But flattery for its own sake usually is."

He chuckled in answer, adding, "You're much too critical of your own attractions."

"Oh, I'm not so falsely modest that I don't realize I'm attractive in my own way," Jolie explained, feeling a stab of pain in her chest for no apparent reason she could determine. "But Helen of Troy I'm not."

"A man wants to make love to a woman, not war over her. A beautiful woman's attractions wane if you constantly have to fight off rivals to prove your love."

"That's a profound statement." An unknown anger darkened her eyes as she secured the lock on the picnic basket and started to rise. "Is that a reverse compliment? Downgrade beauty and upgrade plainness?"

"No, I was only saying that inner beauty is much more attractive than outer beauty."

Now on her feet, Jolie began juggling the different parcels into her arms. The man was complimenting her, but for some reason he was only succeeding in making her feel more inadequate. She had always been very confident and well able to hold her own against any man, except this man. He had too much sex appeal, too overpowering a personality, and was much too handsome for her to let herself be drawn into any lighthearted dalliance with him. Jolie knew he would come out unscathed, but she had serious doubts about herself. It was just as well that she flee now.

"I hope you don't think I share my food and run, but I'd really better be on my way," she smiled, refusing to let the bitter taste in her mouth influence her words of goodbye.

"The afternoon is early." He, too, was on his feet, looking down on her in such a way to make her want to stay.

"But my vacation is short." Regret crept into her sigh.

He reached out and removed the picnic basket from her hand. It put a dent in her ego that he gave up his persuasion so easily, standing back waiting for her to lead the way to her car. Once everything was stowed in the back seat, Jolie turned to say goodbye.

"You should paint spots on the car to match your freckles," a finger brushed her cheek in emphasis. "Then you would both be ladybirds ready to fly away home."

"That would be a novelty, wouldn't it?" she agreed, unable to meet his compelling eyes. She slipped behind the wheel. "Thanks for sharing your fishing hole with me."

"Thanks for the lunch," he returned.

"Well, goodbye." The words sounded artificially bright even to Jolie's ears.

"Not goodbye, *au revoir*. Till we meet again."

Not much chance of that, Jolie thought, as she started the car and drove away. How could they possibly meet again? He didn't know her name or where she lived, and vice versa. And that was a depressing thought.

CHAPTER FIVE

GUY AND his father were attending a meeting of a local men's club. Mrs. LeBlanc was visiting an older relative who was confined to her home. Michelle was sitting on the green plaid-cushioned wicker sofa, school papers spread around her with more that she was correcting on her lap. The record player had an airy instrumental record on its turntable, filling the room with its lighthearted sound.

Jolie was in a matching wicker chair trying to finish the letter she had begun to her Aunt Brigitte, but she couldn't match the jubilant enthusiasm in the previous writing.

A strong, tanned face with raven black hair and contrasting deep blue eyes kept springing to the forefront of her thoughts. It was frustrating that a stranger she would never see again kept coming back to haunt her. It wasn't as if she had never been around men quite as attractive as he, because she had. And while she had admired their looks, she certainly hadn't been sent into the doldrums over them. Why was this one so different? Jolie freely admitted to herself that the stranger had fascinated her with his lore of Louisiana, his ready sense of humor, and the lack of any discernible vanity. He had been confident, but not arrogant, teasing without mocking, and knowing without revealing what he knew. It was ridiculous to keep dwelling on him, she told herself disgustedly. She wasn't a child any more and she was hardly the type to moon over a man whose name she didn't even know. Jolie didn't realize her heaving sigh had been so loud until Michelle's dark eyes had looked up questioningly from behind the gold-rimmed glasses.

"Writing to the boy back home?"

"If I had an ounce of brains, I would be," Jolie grimaced. "But I'm writing to my aunt instead."

"That illogical answer tells me two things," Michelle chuckled. "There is a boy back home and you've evidently split with him."

"Right on both counts."

"Miss him?"

"No, except every now and then when I get an attack of conscience," Jolie admitted, a rueful smile lifting the corners of her mouth for a brief moment.

"He loved you, but you didn't love him. That always makes you feel like a louse." Michelle tapped the papers on her lap into a neat stack and set them with the others on the other half of the couch.

"John was everything a girl looks for in a man—gentle, loving and good-looking. I cared about him a lot, but nothing happened when he kissed me." Jolie laughed at herself, realizing how juvenile that statement sounded. "So I guess I'm still in search of Prince Charming." Inwardly she shouted at the image of the stranger that jumped to mind, ordering him to go away.

"'Lagniappe,'" said Michelle, nodding her head.

"What?"

"'Lagniappe'—'something extra' would be the rough translation. It's a word you see quite often in advertisements of Louisiana," she explained.

The word suited her feelings perfectly, but it didn't give Jolie any more of a clue to what exactly she was looking for.

At the present time, the best solution was to take her aunt's advice and not dwell on the problem, but let the passing of time solve it for her.

"I thought I would drive to Opelousas tomorrow, tour the Jim Bowie museum, then stop in Lafayette," Jolie decided.

The subject was then diverted to the various sights to be seen in the two cities. Yet later, when

Jolie was beneath the covers of her bed, sleep was slow in coming. Despite her attempts to think of her excursion the following morning, her mind kept returning to the day's activities. And very few of her thoughts were conducive to sleep. When it did come, it was a tossing, fitful slumber.

JOLIE HAD set out to exhaust herself mentally and physically on her trip to Opelousas and Lafayette. She had succeeded to the point that she couldn't remember if she had seen that peculiar Steamboat Gothic house with the "widow's walk" in Opelousas or Lafayette before realizing that it had been neither. The house had been in a smaller town called Washington.

Now, the following morning, she practically had to force herself out of the bed. Her sleep had been heavy and she had awoken with the feeling she was drugged. Her mouth felt dry and cottony. Sleep still clung to her heavy-lidded eyes as she slowly descended the stairs.

"Good morning," Mrs. LeBlanc's lilting voice rang out cheerfully.

Jolie looked about her blankly, finally finding the source when she saw Mrs. LeBlanc near the kitchen doorway. If she had been drinking the day before, Jolie didn't think she could have felt much worse than she did at the present moment. With leaden movements, she walked to the kitchen.

"There's some fresh squeezed orange juice in the jug," the woman told her, "and the glasses are in the right-hand cupboard above the sink. What would you like for breakfast?"

"Just some toast and coffee is good enough," said Jolie, retrieving a glass from the cupboard. Stifling a yawn, she poured the orange juice in the glass, eager to rid her mouth of its sleep taste.

"What are your plans for today?" Mrs. LeBlanc asked as she set a plate of toast in front of her and returned to the counter for the coffee.

"None, really. I thought maybe I'd go out to the State Park here in St. Martinville," she replied in between refreshing sips of the citrus drink.

"Good. You remember me speaking about one of our friends who owns an old plantation?"

Jolie struggled for his name. "Etienne?"

"Yes," the older women smiled brightly. "He telephoned yesterday while you were gone. I mentioned you were staying with us and were anxious to see some of the sights around here, and he very generously offered to show you around his place today."

"Today?" Jolie echoed. She really didn't know if she was in the mood to spend time with some talkative elderly Frenchman.

"He suggested that you stop out around ten this morning, before the heat of the day. I never thought to ask him, but he might know something about the plantation you're trying to find."

"Cameron Hall?" Well, that pretty well settled it. Cameron Hall was the reason she had come down here. It would be foolish to pass up the first opportunity to talk to someone who might know about it.

"I told him I was quite sure you'd come. You are, aren't you?" For the first time, Mrs. Le-Blanc noticed Jolie's lack of enthusiasm for the invitation.

"Oh, I'd love to." Jolie managed to shake the sleep away long enough to nod vigorously.

"The Temple, Etienne's plantation, is some miles from town." Mrs. LeBlanc smiled, reassured that Jolie was interested in her friend's invitation. "I'll write down the directions how to get there."

At nine-thirty Jolie set out for Etienne's plantation. Her spirits had still not returned to their previous level of buoyancy. And the imaginary clouds didn't disappear when she discovered that Mrs. LeBlanc's instructions led her in the same direction as the one she had taken the day she met the stranger. She was perversely glad when they finally deviated from her previous course into another section of the countryside. She didn't want to go back to where those blue eyes would haunt her again.

A dirt road branched off to her left bearing the sign "Private Road—No Trespassing." This was it, Jolie sighed, a flicker of interest piercing her boredom now that her destination was near. Mrs. LeBlanc had told her the house would be on her left about a quarter mile from the turn-off on to the dirt road. A dilapidated fence ran parallel with the road. In most places the wire had long since been parted from the posts, but there was little chance that anyone would be able to enter the property that way unless they possessed a machete. A dense growth of vines, shrubbery and spiky palmettoes lay at the feet of a row of pine trees.

No matter how hard Jolie attempted to peer through the tangled growth, all she was able to see was a glimpse of something large and white. It had to be the plantation, but it was invisible from the road. Two crumbling white pillars marked the entrance which was blocked by padlocked iron grillework gates.

It was beginning to become obvious to her that prosperity had turned its back on this plantation. She was also beginning to wonder what kind of an eccentric character this Etienne would turn out to be.

Parking her Volkswagen on the side of the narrow lane, Jolie got out and walked over to the gate, looking through the bars trying to see some sign of life. The place looked deserted. Then she spied the bell suspended on the side of one of the pillars. She pulled the rope attached to it and the strident ding-dong rang shrilly in the stillness. That harsh, unmelodic sound had to rouse someone, Jolie thought, walking over to stand in front of the gate.

There was a sudden rustle of brush, followed by a whirlwind sound coming toward her. Suddenly she was staring into the bared, snarling white fangs of a dog, his front feet on the gate until he was eye-level with her. Her heart was in her throat. Her feet were rooted to the ground as she stared at the growling German Shepherd, black as a midnight sky without moon or stars. This was hardly the greeting or greeter that she had anticipated. Although why she should be surprised at anything connected with this derelict plantation, she didn't know.

Mobility finally returned to her as she realized that the dog couldn't get beyond the gate. She didn't intend to stick around to see what Mr. Etienne who-ever-he-was was like. She was going back to St. Martinville. Just as she turned toward her car, a voice rang out clear and commanding.

"Black, heel!"

Jolie turned back in time to see the dog's snarling mouth change into a laughing grin as he came down on all fours. With a wagging tale, he reversed his direction and raced toward the man just coming into view. Jolie stared incredulously as he gave the dog a rewarding pat before continuing toward her. It was the stranger from the bayou!

"I hope you'll forgive Black's greeting." His smile danced out at her, highlighted by the audacious twinkle in his blue eyes. "He isn't accustomed to strangers, even if they are attractive young ladies."

"I came...." The words stuck in her throat as she continued to gaze at him in a mixture of bewildered astonishment. "Y-you're... you're Etienne?"

"At your service, Miss Jolie Antoinette Smith." As his head dipped in a bow, his dark hair glistened as blackly as the dog's.

"But how... I mean... did you know?" She was stammering like a schoolgirl.

"I was fairly certain I recognized the picnic basket and Josephine's touch with the food. My phone call confirmed it."

The gate was unlocked and swung open to admit her. Now that the initial surprise had passed, Jolie felt a heady feeling overtake her as she realized that Etienne had sought her out. And her own pleasure at finding him again was revealed in her sparkling brown eyes. She stepped past the barred gate, stopping just inches inside as a question suddenly occurred to her.

"Why didn't you tell Mrs. LeBlanc you'd already met me the day before?"

He had closed the gate behind her and stood so close to her she was almost touching him. His nearness almost took her breath away, especially when she looked into the unfathomable expression in his dancing blue eyes.

"Why didn't you?" he countered smoothly, asking the question in such a way that Jolie felt he already knew the answer.

"I didn't have your advantage of being able to deduce where you were staying." The faintest blush of pink touched her cheeks before Jolie was able to step away from his disturbing nearness. "Besides, how would it have sounded if I'd told her about that afternoon?" she laughed hesitantly. "How could I have said, 'Mrs. LeBlanc, I shared my picnic lunch with this man today. He had dark hair, vivid blue eyes, somewhere in his thirties, but I don't know what his name was'? That would have sounded just a little bit strange."

"Not strange." He shook his head at her and smiled. "A bit forward for you, perhaps, which is why I almost didn't call."

"Didn't call? Why?" Confusion knitted her forehead as Etienne took her arm and began leading her down the narrow path towards the plantation.

"In the past, it's always been my policy to stay away from spirited virgins. They tend to complicate your life . . . and your conscience."

For only a moment did the stabbing hurt flicker in her eyes before Jolie concealed it, damning the look of innocence she had been born with. She knew his gaze was dwelling on her. If he had any doubts about his verdict that she was a virgin, her own reaction had confirmed it.

"Then why did you bother?" she asked stiffly, riveting her gaze on the overgrown path they were walking.

"I haven't decided. It was an impulse, I guess."

His hand tightened on her arm, checking her stride and bringing her to a halt beside him. Jolie stared down at his polished black shoes and his ivory white slacks. Gathering courage, she raised her eyes past the silk shirt with its large white flowers etched against a background of bright blue that intensified the color of his eyes gazing into her own. He was every inch the commanding plantation owner.

"But, Jolie," she couldn't stop the tingle of pleasure tickling the back of her neck at the quiet way he said her name, "I'm glad that I gave in to that impulse."

She wanted to say that she was glad, too, but it would have been too revealing of her own budding feelings for this man. To deny that she was would have been an outright lie, and Etienne was much too perceptive not to know. Since nothing she could say would be right, she didn't reply at all.

"Are you sorry you came?" Etienne asked.

With his thoughtful gaze observing every nuance of her expression, she didn't bother to lie. "I'm not sorry I came," she replied easily, summoning all her pride to meet his scrutiny without flinching.

A ghost of a smile teased the corners of his mouth. "You're remarkable. Honesty is not usually a virtue found in women."

"Nor in men." Jolie immediately regretted the sharpness that had been in her answering retort.

A throaty chuckle accompanied his full flashing white smile and Jolie felt the warmth flooding her cheeks. She quickly resumed walking, too conscious of the man beside her.

"Your tongue has barbs." The laughing sound was still in Etienne's voice. "I think we're going to have a very enjoyable day, Black."

His teasing words were addressed to the German Shepherd padding contentedly beside him. Jolie's glittering brown eyes cast a venomous look at his confident expression, angered that he was so sure of her attraction to him. His gaze caught the look, his blue eyes deflecting the daggers with amusement. Jolie determinedly looked away from him, forcing her attention ahead of her.

The dense growth had thinned without Jolie being aware of it. Her steps faltered, then ceased altogether as an unobstructed view spread out before her. Dominating the scene rose a mansion of such colossal proportions that it took Jolie's breath away. Immense pillars surrounded the square building, supporting a second floor balcony as well as the heavy cornice crown of the flat roof. Yet its height was so awesome that Jolie couldn't begin to guess how tall it was. Shutters of dark green accented the floor-to-ceiling windows on each floor and complemented the exterior that had weathered to a pale yellow with age, while patches of flaking paint indicated the wooden railings on the upper balcony had once been white.

In spite of the blemishes that had accumulated on the more than century-old structure, there was still that undefinable air of majesty about it. The severity of its heavy Greek architecture gave it an almost regal dignity that carried it through, even in the face of partial deterioration. Overpowering, palatial, stately, all the adjectives that sprang to Jolie's mind seemed to be inadequate.

Adding to its magnificence, the plantation was surrounded by oak trees of the size and girth that astounded Jolie regardless of how many times she had seen them in her few trips in the area. Their branches were the size of a normal tree trunk, here and there dipping so close to the ground that a person could sit on them as if they were a chair. As always, their leafy arms were draped with greenish-gray Spanish moss, turning the gnarled giants into picturesque wise old men with flowing gray beards.

Jolie finally tore her gaze away from the impressive scene, her dazzled expression turning toward Etienne. He was smiling at her gently, sympathetically aware of how moving a sight the plantation was.

"The Temple always affects a stranger that way," he said, when she could still find no words to express herself.

"It is like a temple," she breathed, shifting her gaze back to the mansion. "How lucky you are to own it."

"She owns me." Etienne smiled ruefully, his gaze following Jolie's as his hand moved to the small of her back and they resumed their walk toward the mansion. "And she's a much more demanding mistress than any one woman I've ever known. I saw her for the first time four years ago. A year later I gave in and bought her."

"I thought the Temple was your family's home, that it had been passed down to you through generations," Jolie glanced at him in slight surprise.

"If it had, I would never have allowed it to get into the state she was in when I bought her. She was being used as a cattle barn." Jolie didn't have to see his face to know that anger was lurking just below the surface. And she agreed with him, her stomach knotting at such irreverence.

Five steps led to the wooden porch and the enormous double door leading inside. Jolie noticed the new sections of planking that had replaced rotting boards on the porch as Etienne opened one of the doors and waited for her to precede him into the interior of the house. At first the dimness was acute, then her eyes adjusted to the absence of the glaring sunlight. A coolness assailed her as she gazed about her.

"The walls are approximately two feet thick and keep the temperature at about seventy-four degrees year round,'' Etienne explained when she shivered slightly at the sudden drop in temperature.

The wide hallway split the house in half with another set of double doors leading outside directly ahead of Jolie. On one side of the hallway there were four doors, and three doors and an oval spiral staircase were on the other side. With the exception of a table in the hallway, the place was barren of any furnishings. Etienne grasped her elbow and guided her farther down the hall.

''All the floors in the downstairs had been destroyed by the cattle. I just had them replaced last winter.'' His eyes were an even darker shade of blue when he glanced at her. She knew their glittering darkness was for the mistreatment of the house.

Jolie followed silently as he pointed out the butler's pantry, the large room—equivalent to the present day living room, the dining room, the office where the plantation owner directed the day's activities and maintained his records, and a smaller room used as a sitting room-parlor. All the rooms were without furniture and in various stages of re-finishing. Jolie noted the harsh lines about his face as he explained that the carved fireplaces in each room had been vandalized and were beyond restoration. New ones were being constructed, but she sensed his indignation that the beauty of the originals was never again to be appreciated by anyone.

"We can be thankful that cattle never showed any inclination for stairs." Etienne smiled, leading her back to the staircase. "Because this mansion possesses a magnificent one. A self-supporting oval spiral, the steps are made of cypress and the carved balustrades are mahogany. There are no nails. Each post is individually fitted to the stairs and railing."

The wood still maintained its luster and was satiny smooth to the touch. Jolie couldn't resist letting her hand trail along its surface as they climbed the steps to the second floor. Here the fireplaces in the bedrooms were untouched, although they did show signs of neglect, except for one that Etienne had cleaned, restained and varnished. There was more furniture, too, but most of it had too many layers of dirt for its beauty to be seen. He showed her an exceptionally old armoire, explaining that clothes were not hung on hangers, but folded and placed in the drawers contained behind the doors of the tall forerunner of the present-day chest of drawers.

Then he led her back into the hallway which was a duplicate of the one downstairs, dividing the second floor into equal parts with double doors at each end leading on to the upper gallery. It was through one of these doors that Jolie was taken and the view was breathtaking. It took her a few minutes to realize that she was at the opposite side from which she had entered the house and looking at the rear lawns. A ribbon of shining water winked at her beyond more clusters of giant oaks and magnolias.

"Is that a pond down there?" She turned excitedly to Etienne, who was also gazing over his land with a proprietorial air.

"That's Bayou Teche. Roads were practically nonexistent in the old days. All plantations were close to one bayou or another since they were the major routes of transportation, just as the first plantations followed the Mississippi River so they would have ready access to transport their products," he explained. "The waterways were the roads in early day Louisiana."

Jolie nodded, realizing the logic of it. She started to look back to the lawns when a thought suddenly occurred to her.

"You didn't show me the kitchens. Where are they?"

"The fear of fire was too great for them to ever be in the main house." Etienne smiled at her strictly feminine question. "I found some foundations that I think were probably for the kitchen near the north side, not far from the dining room."

"Where do you live?" The dancing gleam sprang quickly into his eyes at her impulsive question. It momentarily flustered her. "I mean, you obviously can't...well, live in the house. Not yet, anyway."

"Come." He reached out and took her hand, the warmth of his touch sending tremors through her. "I'll show you where I live."

CHAPTER SIX

ETIENNE LED her back downstairs and out the same door they had entered. Then he turned to the left, instead of taking the path leading to her car. As they rounded the mansion, Jolie spied a petite version of the Temple.

"It's a miniature replica of the house!" she exclaimed in delight.

"Commonly known as the garçonnière where the younger or unmarried male members of the family resided. *Garçon* is the French word for boy." He released her hand to open the screen door, then brought it back to her shoulder as he escorted her inside.

It was only one large room with stairs leading to the second floor and a lace grillework partition sectioning off the kitchen area. The furnishings were simple, all functional, and completely masculine. The pressure of his hand guided Jolie farther into the room. She felt like a fly being lured by a spider. She was slowly being spun into a web that she couldn't escape.

"Would you like a cold drink?" Etienne's voice had taken on a seductive quality, its caressing softness coming from somewhere near her ear. Or was it only her imagination interpreting it to be so? The hand left her shoulder as Etienne stepped away from her toward the kitchen. Jolie walked hesitantly about the small room, too conscious of their isolation to feel comfortable. It suddenly seemed so terribly improper to be in Etienne's house, which was really ridiculous considering how she had roamed John Talbot's house at will. Yet the feeling of intimacy continued to wrap itself about her.

"Lemonade." Etienne held out a glass to her.

Warily Jolie glanced up to his eyes that had narrowed at the slight trembling in her hand when she had taken the glass. His dark, curling lashes shadowed the blueness of his eyes.

"Perhaps we should sit outside. You might be more comfortable there."

Now he mocked her, but Jolie seized the suggestion anyway. Once outside in the lawn chairs, conversation lagged. Etienne seemed content to gaze at the house that dominated the scenery, his eyes occasionally straying about the lawn. Jolie took the opportunity to study him. Since their previous meeting, he had changed. He wasn't quite the same person she had met, or thought she had met.

There was still the same litheness of movement, the instinctive grace of an athlete. The unnaturally dark blue eyes still gleamed with amusement and the smile was just as ready to show the grooves deepening near his mouth. Yet before Etienne had given her the impression of indolence, laziness, a devil-may-care approach to life. And today—today Jolie had seen something else. The purposeful set of his jaw, the finely chiseled, slightly aristocratic nose that could flare with distaste, the blue eyes that flickered with burning anger, and the overwhelming strength that emanated like an aura around him. But she was struck not only by his inborn dignity, but also by his iron-willed determination that indicated he might be quite ruthless if it was required.

"Have you decided whether I can be trusted?" His face was turned away from her. His strong profile was etched against the backdrop of trees. Yet he had been completely aware of her scrutiny.

"I think," Jolie fought back the briefly rising flush of embarrassment, "that if you put a gold ring in your ear, you would make an excellent pirate."

"From some women that might be a compliment." Now he turned to study her and Jolie avoided meeting his penetrating gaze. "What a pity I'm only a poor plantation owner."

"The best things in life are free," Jolie quipped, seeking a lighter topic.

"Don't you believe it!" The sound that accompanied his derisive words was a combination of laughter and disdain. "You pay dearly for everything in one way or another."

"And what is the price for love?" The cynical tone in his voice startled her.

"The most precious thing a man has, his freedom." His eyes were harsh and piercing as he glanced over at her.

"Are you one of those exasperating men who are determined to be confirmed bachelors?" Jolie laughed, not at all sure just how she should take his remarks.

"Are you one of those exasperating women who believe happiness ends in marriage?" he retorted.

"Yes and no." Her chin tilted upward in bright defiance. "I believe happiness begins in love and continues in marriage, but I'm a dyed-in-the-wool romantic."

"You're truthful." A quirk of his eyebrows revealed his amusement. "Tell me, what is love?"

Jolie breathed in sharply, then slowly exhaled as she turned her gaze outward toward the bright sunlight bathing the house in a deeper yellow glow.

"I don't know. I've never been in love. What about you?"

"Many times." The full force of his magnetic blue eyes were turned on her and she felt the full power of his virility. "Which is why I don't believe it."

"If your freedom is so precious to you, why did you tie yourself down to this plantation? You said yourself that it's more demanding than any woman."

"You listen to what a man says. That's another rare trait." His gaze moved over her slowly. "I was tired of traveling, of not having any roots. And this place bore my name."

"I don't understand." She tilted her head questioningly at him.

"I'll show you," he laughed, sitting his glass on the tiled porch floor of the garçonnière, and Jolie did the same.

His arm slipped around her waist as he assisted her down the narrow steps of the porch. Jolie felt her throat tightening at his easy intimacy that she couldn't match with the same degree of indifference. Etienne puzzled her; he was an enigma. She couldn't help wondering what had happened to him that had made him so wary of women. No, he wasn't wary; he was disillusioned. Of course, a man with his enormous attractiveness would gather women like flies to honey. Perhaps in his case, familiarity bred contempt.

"If you felt the need to settle down, then haven't you ever wished for children of your own?" Jolie asked, finding the silence of their stroll led her thoughts in channels she wasn't prepared to take yet. Besides, the arm around her shoulder was much too disturbing for coherent thought.

Her stomach somersaulted as Etienne looked down on her, his eyes resting on her lips a little too long for her peace of mind. What was worse, Jolie couldn't help wondering what it would be like if he kissed her. She had guessed from the beginning that he would be very experienced in the art of making love.

"Children aren't just a product of marriage."

There was such wickedness in his smile that Jolie knew he was attempting to shock her.

"It's convenient for the child if it is," keeping her voice calm, not reacting to his taunt.

"Spoken very properly."

Etienne halted their strolling pace, his hand squeezing her arm in an unspoken order to remain where she was while he walked to a flowering shrub and broke off one of the large white blooms. He walked back to her, bringing the petals to his nose to sniff the fragrance before offering it to Jolie. As her fingers closed over his hand to take the short stem, he didn't immediately release it, forcing her hand to linger with his.

"Virtue should always be rewarded," he said in a husky, drawling voice that enveloped her in his virility. A little rosy hue stole over her face when he finally released it and she tried to hide it in a silent appreciation of the velvet smoothness of the petals.

She stole a glance at his face through the veil of her lashes. A suppressed smile was on his face that was now turned ahead of them. It hurt to discover that her lack of sophistication amused him. His arm was back around her waist, guiding her closer toward the shining mirror of water.

A pillar, aging and pockmarked, stood forlornly near the water. Its mate lay in a rubble of bricks and stucco in the tall grass. Here along the bayou was the front entrance to the plantation that had once matched the gates Jolie had entered but now had fallen to ruin. Etienne led her to the one standing pillar.

"This is what led to my final decision that the Fates wanted me to buy the house," he said quietly.

At his curious statement, Jolie followed his solemn gaze to the pillar. Amidst the gouges of time there were fading letters carved into the standing pillar. They were so faint that it took some time for Jolie to make out the word. There was a sudden tightening in her chest as the significance registered.

"Cameron!" she breathed so softly that it was barely audible, blinking hard to make sure the word was not a figment of her imagination. It wasn't. She stared back at the mansion, standing in all its regal glory amidst the giant oaks before turning to Etienne, tears of exultation filling her brown eyes.

"I've found it!" Her voice squeaked with emotion. "I've found Cameron Hall!"

Her hands reached out for his as her happiness bubbled over. Her delight bewildered him and she managed to control her exuberance long enough to give him the sketchy details. The wonder of her discovery wiped away the reserve that she had erected in defence of his masculinity. When Etienne joined in with her happiness, Jolie found herself slipping quite easily into his arms.

"Can you believe it?" she exclaimed, letting her arms twine around him as they stared at the name etched on the pillar. Her head leaned naturally against his broad chest as she sighed her happiness. "No one I questioned had ever heard of Cameron Hall. I was afraid I would never find it." Her voice was husky and emotion-filled. "And now I find your home is it."

She raised her head to gaze into his eyes, her face radiant with the thrilling discovery. She sensed more than felt Etienne catch his breath as he looked down upon her, his eyes turning a darker shade of blue. And she became conscious of the pressure of his thighs against her, the muscular hardness of his chest, and the firm caress of his hands on her back and shoulders. Her heart skipped a beat, then accelerated. She felt Etienne's arms tighten about her. The sensuous curve of his lips moved nearer.

Jolie knew she should break her gaze away from the hypnotic darkness of his eyes, but it was impossible. His head had to bend quite a distance to reach her lips and Etienne didn't hurry to close the gap. Jolie felt as if she was on the brink of another discovery. "Lagniappe." The word danced in her thoughts.

Then his lips were on hers, soft and gentle like the petals on the flower he had given her. The tenseness that had held Jolie immobilized melted away in the flood of warmth as his lips moved persuasively against hers. There was no thought of resistance, so she simply responded. Her yielding brought an added possessiveness to his kiss that sent tremors quaking through her body. When Etienne dragged his mouth from hers and brought his hands up to cup the face she would have turned away, Jolie felt cheated. That she had just been given something beautiful and it had been taken away. The disappointment was mirrored in her clouded brown eyes.

"I've been wanting to do that from the first moment I saw you." His face was only inches away from hers.

She had moved her hands from his back to rest against his chest. She intended to disentangle herself from his embrace, but the feel of his heart thudding against her hand stopped her. The roughness of his thumb caressed her lips, parting them slightly before he claimed them again. This time there was no gentle exploration as Jolie's arms wound around his neck in artless abandon, succumbing to the desire to let her fingers curl into his black hair. The flame that blazed within her seemed to be in him too. His arms moved to her back, arching her against him in an attempt to fuse them together.

A moan escaped her lips when his mouth deserted hers to ravage her ear lobe and the pulsating cord in her neck. A curious ringing sound was in her ears as the ache to have his lips on hers became too much to bear. She was crushed so tightly against him that she couldn't breathe, but breath didn't seem to be necessary to life. This was "lagniappe," the something extra she had been looking for all her life. Then his hands moved to her arms, firmly drawing them from around his neck to hold them tightly against his chest.

Jolie couldn't bring herself to meet his gaze, feeling a spark of shame that she had responded much too openly to his kisses. She stared instead at the darkly tanned hands that clasped hers, experiencing a thrill at the ragged breathing that said Etienne had not been untouched by the passionate embrace.

"Do I thank you or your ancestor for that?" Etienne asked softly.

Peering up at him, Jolie saw his eyes still glittering beneath the partially closed lids. She knew a sudden desire for experience that should have enabled her to make some witty rejoinder. After one embrace, it was idiotic to tell a man you were falling in love with him.

"Both," she ended in whispering.

"Stay to lunch with me." His hands tightened on hers as if challenging her to disobey the order.

She had the impression that if she refused he would sweep her into his arms again and kiss her until she relented. She hesitated, wondering whether she didn't want him to do just that.

"Jolie," Etienne murmured, and she felt his body straining toward her. Her vulnerability was too great. Another tempestuous embrace like the last and she might agree to anything.

"I'd like to stay." She swallowed convulsively as she looked into his face.

The very look in his eyes told her she had been right in thinking he would have had his way in one manner or another. She hadn't real-

ized the tenseness that had been between them
until Etienne relaxed, bringing one of her hands
up to his mouth where he brushed her palm with
a kiss.

"At the moment, food is farthest from my
mind," he sighed with a half smile as he turned
Jolie until she was nestled under his arm. He
held her so closely against him that it made
walking difficult, but Jolie didn't mind.

They retraced their steps toward the plantation. Jolie couldn't help thinking that the big
house was looking down at them with satisfaction. She breathed in deeply, drinking in every
scent and sound that surrounded this happiest
of all moments. Not only had she discovered
Cameron Hall, but Etienne as well, and a smile
as golden as the sun radiated from her face.
When they entered the tiny replica of the plantation, Etienne pulled her again into his arms.

"Is it really necessary that we feed that hunger now?"

Jolie felt the warmth spreading through her
loins at the lean hardness of his body against
her. Her resolve to remain level-headed was
nearly swept away with the fiery desire for his
kiss.

"We...we should, yes." Her breathy stam-
mer wasn't too convincing. Blue eyes narrowed
on her face that tried to remain composed.

"You're right, of course." The rueful grimace was meant to appear playful, but Jolie caught the fleeting glimpse of repressed anger.

"Etienne?" Her hand touched his arm to stop him when he moved away from her. He stared down at her puzzled expression that couldn't understand what she had done to upset him.

"Don't look at me like that." There was no softness in his face. "I might not win the next battle with my conscience, and you've already destroyed my peace of mind."

Her question was answered and Jolie was appropriately subdued. She recognized that he was a man who seldom settled for chaste kisses and unless she wanted to deal with the consequences, she had best let him lead the way. Something in her expression must have mirrored her wavering confidence, because Etienne lifted her drooping chin and planted a kiss on her lips.

"I forgot to tell you," he smiled. His mood changed with quicksilver rapidity. "You have to help fix lunch."

"Oh, I'm very good at that." Jolie adopted his lighter mood quickly. "I have a diploma in home economics."

"I'm impressed. We must definitely put that training to use." Etienne walked to the refrigerator and opened the door. "What would a home economics graduate make out of lettuce, leftover ham, boiled eggs and tomatoes? Something tasty, I hope, since that's the sum total of my food.''

She laughed easily now. ''If you're able to conjure up some oil and vinegar and some spices, I might be able to make us a chef's salad.''

''That's my speciality,'' he assured her. ''Leave the dressing to me.''

Jolie never did discover exactly how Etienne prepared the dressing, since she was busy with her own chores. But one taste of the delicately flavored dressing had whetted the appetite she didn't think she possessed. Etienne very wisely turned their conversation to his plans for the restoration of the plantation. Although Jolie was interested, every now and then she found herself studying the gleam of his black hair in the sunlight or the sharp contrast his blue eyes made to the darkness of the rest of his features and ended up catching only snatches of his plans. Just looking at his strikingly handsome face and feeling the masculinity that emanated from him sent Jolie reeling, unable to believe that he could be attracted to her.

''...On rainy days, I've been refinishing the wood on a Victorian sofa and two matching chairs,'' he was saying, swirling the white wine that accompanied their meal. ''One more coat of varnish and the sofa will be finished, except for reupholstering, which I'll have to pay dearly to have done."

"Upholstery?" Jolie exclaimed. The familar subject caught her attention. "It's a hobby of mine."

Etienne glanced up sharply, causing her to blush. She hadn't meant to force him into a position of asking her to help.

"I'm . . . I'm really quite good at it," she said quickly. "I used to earn money for college doing it."

"I don't doubt that you're capable. I remembered you saying you were only here on vacation. It just occurred to me that you would be leaving."

An inexpressible surge of joy swelled her chest as she realized his tight-lipped expression had nothing to do with upholstering, but her eventual departure. He did care for her.

"I planned to stay for three weeks." It was hard keeping her voice calm. "Or until my money ran out."

"I could pay you for your time." A dangerous light glittered in his eyes. "If it would keep you here longer."

"You might regret that offer," Jolie laughed tightly, her hands toying with her glass of wine.

Etienne hesitated before replying. "It would be a shame if you had to leave when you've only just found Cameron Hall."

"And you? What about you?" Jolie thought silently, wondering why he had chosen his words with such care. He obviously didn't want to commit himself. Just because she felt so sure of her feeling toward him did not make the reverse true. He found her physically attractive, of that he had left her in no doubt. But he was a man, and love was not a necessary emotion to them when it came to making love. Or at least, not to the same degree as it was to a woman. Besides, he had already told her he didn't believe in love.

Nervousness captured her hands. She quickly busied them stacking the dishes to carry them to the porcelain sink. She knew Etienne was watching her intently, but she didn't know what to say. It was beyond her previous experience. She grasped at the one subject that led down the middle road.

"I'm glad Cameron Hall hasn't been restored," keeping her voice light as she carried the dishes to the sink. "There's more atmosphere of how it was long ago than if it were filled with priceless antiques. That sounds contradictory, doesn't it?"

She turned to address her question to Etienne, whom she had left sitting at the small table, only to find him standing directly behind her. He was towering over her, making her feel like an insignificant dwarf. The feeling was intensified by the enigmatic expression that had darkened his eyes.

"You're a domestic creature." His blunt words brought a flicker of pain in her eyes. She couldn't believe his eyes could look so cold. "Marriage has never been a part of my plans, Jolie."

"What am I supposed to say to that?" She swallowed at the tears trying to spring forward.

"Nothing." The retort was sharp and clipped while his gaze burned its cold fire over her face. "I didn't want any pretense raising its ugly head."

"However I may look, I'm not a child!" Temper rising quickly to defend her.

A corner of his mouth lifted in a half smile. "No, you're all woman—I've discovered that." That powerful magnetic charm reached out to pull Jolie beneath his spell. She started to move around him, ostensibly to gather the rest of the dishes, but an arm shot out to block the way.

"And in spite of my common sense that tells me to get you out of here before I hurt you, I keep thinking of reasons for you to stay."

His voice was a caressing whisper against her hair as he moved closer, pinioning her against the sink. Jolie felt her knees weakening and knew that if her hands let go of the counter top they would find their way around his neck. She forced herself to turn around, staring at the dirty dishes in the sink.

"Did you know 'Jolie' translates into 'pretty' in French?" he asked huskily.

"And Etienne," she gulped, his closeness cutting off her breath. "What does it translate to?"

"Steven." His mouth found the hollow between her shoulder and her neck. Jolie groaned and moved so swiftly away from him that he was unable to check her flight.

"I don't even know your name." A sudden stab of something akin to fear pierced her heart. Wild panic trembled over her as she remembered Michelle and Guy speaking of a man named Steve.

He was looking at her with puzzled wariness. "Surely Josep...Mrs. LeBlanc told you who I am? Cameron, my name is Steve Cameron."

"She called you Etienne," Jolie said quietly, realizing there could not be another man that would fit Michelle's warning phrase— Fire burns and if you get too near Steve you get scorched. The LeBlanc family considered him to be staked out as Claudine LeBlanc's property.

"She's always called me Etienne," he concluded.

CHAPTER SEVEN

PIECES OF the puzzle began to rain on Jolie's head, forming a picture she wasn't sure she could figure out. Guy had referred to Steve as a very formidable opponent. That was an understatement, considering the way her defenses had collapsed under his very first advance. Steve Cameron. No wonder the name Cameron on the pillar had persuaded him to buy the plantation!

Through the haze of her racing thoughts, Jolie looked at Etienne who was now Steve Cameron. How could she have been so obtuse not to realize that this extremely masculine male had to be the one Guy and Michelle had described? He was watching her calmly, exhibiting only the slightest interest in her bewilderment.

"I feel very foolish." An embarrassed laugh accompanied her words. "Guy and Michelle mentioned you—as Steve, but when Mrs. LeBlanc talked about Etienne, I pictured an elderly man. Even after I met you, I didn't put two and two together until just now."

"I can understand Guy wanting to protect his claim, but why Michelle?" Although the question was asked, Jolie had the feeling he wasn't the slightest bit interested in the answer as his gaze roved over her thoughtfully.

"Guy has no claim on me." She hated the knowing smile that sprang to his mouth. He knew that already. "I merely asked Michelle about you because she was there when Guy mentioned you. She only described you. Not physically, but—"

"Don't tell me Michelle considers me to be a dangerous person?" he chuckled, leaning back against the counter with a complacent expression on his face.

"Not to her," Jolie said quickly.

"Am I dangerous to you?" The blue eyes darkened with his seductively soft words.

Danger meant harm. Did he have the ability to hurt her? She was so close to falling in love with him without assurances that he even cared for her as anything other than a female willing to reciprocate his passion. Yes, Steve Cameron was dangerous to her, but that would be revealing too much of her own feelings to admit it.

"Don't be silly. I know you wouldn't physically harm me." The half truth sprang easily to her lips as she quickly began gathering the rest of the dishes from the table. "Did...did Mrs. LeBlanc tell you that Claudine was coming home this Saturday?"

"Yes, she mentioned it," he replied with marked indifference, taking the dishes from her and placing them in the sink with the others. "Leave them," he ordered. "I want your opinion on the furniture I'm refinishing."

Jolie's lips compressed tightly at his adept shifting of the conversation from his personal life. She was no more knowledgeable about his relationship with Claudine than she had been before. *I may be inexperienced,* Jolie thought determinedly, *but I'm not a shy, retiring little country girl who can be put off so easily.*

"I understand you and Claudine are quite close?" Defiantly she raised her chin so he could see the glint of determination in her eyes as he led her out of the garçonnière.

If she had expected him to be taken aback by her directness, she was mistaken. If anything, Steve Cameron was amused.

"You can thank Claudine for me being here," he said cryptically.

"What do you mean?"

"I met her in New Orleans and she invited me to visit her parents, which I did—with Claudine along, naturally. It was during that visit that she brought me out here to have a picnic while she did some sketchings of the plantation. Later I bought the place."

Jolie didn't have the nerve to ask if it was because of Claudine. "What do you do for a living?"

"I live," he shrugged, the grooves deepening around his mouth at Jolie's wide-eyed expression. "I raise sugar cane which brings in enough money to keep the mortgage up to date and make a few improvements in the house. There's a vegetable garden that grows all the year round and I have a milk cow that faithfully gives me a calf to butcher each year. I'm not plagued with any ambitions for power and wealth. Does that disappoint you?"

"No. You just appear to be the type that could succeed at anything. Commanding others would come natural to you."

Her answer hardened his features, highlighting the hint of ruthlessness around his mouth that had once led her to associate him with the pirates of the old days.

"The furniture is in here." He adeptly avoided commenting on her statement as he opened the large door of a weatherworn building.

Jolie didn't have the opportunity to pursue the subject further because Steve steered the conversation to the furniture. His technical questions made it quite clear that he was knowledgeable in reupholstering. And Jolie was thankful that she could reply intelligently. It was strange how important it was to her for him to think well of her and her abilities.

When they had strolled out of the small building, Steve had given Jolie the go-ahead to pick out samples of material that they could go over together. Yet, even though she was certain of seeing him again, the intimacy that had encircled them was gone. Steve was urbane and charming, just as he had been the first time she had met him, but there seemed to be nothing personal in his attentions. And despite all this pleasure she felt just being in his company, Jolie wanted to reach out and capture again that which they had had.

No matter where they walked the plantation dominated the scene, rising majestically before them. As Jolie and Steve paused near a low-hanging branch of one of the giant oaks, her gaze was drawn to it again while her restless fingers played with a lacelike bunch of Spanish moss.

"Do you really think they lived as luxuriously and as grandly as we've heard?" Jolie sighed. "Were they really wealthy?"

"The life was certainly not all juleps and siestas," Steve replied. "Not if the master of the plantation wanted to own it the following year. The men were entrepreneurs who had many facets of their plantations to control and manipulate in order to achieve the lucrative returns from sugar. Two crop failures and he'd be out of business. If he was successful for a couple of seasons, he had himself a little empire.''

"A sugar king," Jolie mused, and a dimpling smile followed the fanciful thought.

"You must remember plantation owners were few. More than two-thirds of the population in Louisiana at that time owned no slaves at all. But the Grand Manner is much more colorful reading than the futile struggles of the poor.''

"You make me feel guilty for admiring the life-style of the plantation owners.'' She glanced at him, chagrin showing on her face.

"You shouldn't," he smiled. "You're young. What's more romantic than imagining the halcyon days of the plantations? It was rugged individualists who built their empires, carved them out of this semitropical wilderness. They simply enjoyed the fruits of their labor to the fullest. Slave labor was a common practice in that era all over the world in one guise or another.''

"I guess that's true," Jolie agreed. "England had its child abuse and the coal mines. Czarist Russia and Europe had their serfs. And the nobility of other countries had their forms of slavery.''

"We have merely had a harder time absorbing our former slaves because of the color distinction.'' The blueness of his eyes sparkled down at her. "Which has led the subject far away from your first question when you wondered whether the plantation owners really did have silver and gold doorknobs and if they tossed silver dollars at the bubbles behind the paddle-wheel of a riverboat. That was what you wanted to hear, wasn't it."

Jolie nodded sheepishly. "I...I...can't help wondering how true they were, especially when you compare them with the hardships of the others."

"You can rest assured that the stories were true, no matter how extravagant they sound. In one household, it was customary to stop all the clocks when a guest arrived so that while he or she was there time would stand still in the joy of the moment, and they wouldn't be started again until that guest had left, whether it be a day, week or month later. Outdoing each other seemed to be a game to plantation owners, and not just in the opulence of their homes, but in hospitality as well. For instance, when a slave brought the breakfast tray to a female guest in the mornings, a full-bloomed rose was placed on the pillow beside her. If the woman didn't waken then, the servant would draw it gently beneath her nose until she did. Then the women would be served a *petit noir* of coffee to wake the body. The host believed her spirit had been awakened by the rose."

"What a beautiful thought!"

"Probably one of the best tales of the extravagance of plantation owners took place near here. Would you like to hear it?" Steve looked down on her indulgently as she nodded eagerly that she would. "A Monsieur Charles Durand owned a plantation on Bayou Teche a few miles outside of St. Martinville. He was quite a colorful character. His first wife had twelve children before she died. He swore on her grave he would never marry again, but within a year he was wed. He wanted to be completely fair to the woman, so they too had twelve children. Monsieur Durand was an unusual man; therefore when two of his daughters accepted marriage proposals from native Louisiana families, the local people expected him to indulge in his usual opulent creativity for the double wedding. He had his slaves go to the woods near Catahoula, Louisiana and trap large spiders. A few days before the wedding he had them set loose among the avenue of trees leading to the main house. The trees soon became a network of lacy webs and on the morning of the wedding, slaves were sent out with bellows and silver and gold dust which they sprayed upon the webs, turning the avenue into a shimmering gossamer canopy for the bridal parties."

"Is that true?" A disbelieving laugh escaped her lips.

"I swear." Steve mockingly crossed his heart to give impetus to the story.

"What if it had rained? Or the wind had blown?" She bit her lip at the thought of such a calamity occurring to destroy the unbelievable decorations!

"On Monsieur Durand's wedding preparations! It wouldn't dare!" He was laughing at her wide-eyed expression, but Jolie didn't mind.

"I'm glad it didn't," she sighed wistfully, trying to visualize what the massive oaks surrounding Cameron Hall would look like glittering with silver and gold.

"Do you realize it's after three, almost four o'clock?" he asked gently.

Jolie turned toward him with a start, suddenly feeling gauche and awkward. She could feel the rising warmth spreading up her neck. It didn't seem possible that the time could have gone by so swiftly.

"I'd ... I'd b ... better be go ... going," she stammered, embarrassment making her fumble for words.

She brushed nervously at her skirt, averting her face from his amused eyes. But when she would have stepped away toward the tangled lane leading to the car, her wrist was caught by him. There was a throaty laugh as he pulled her toward him.

"I don't care if you stay all night." The fire in his eyes sent her pulse leaping. "As a matter of fact, I would prefer it. But I wouldn't like to get into Josephine's black book."

Jolie was more flustered than before. "I . . . I'm sure sh . . . she expects me back for dinner this evening." She couldn't meet that virile gaze. "I'm glad you reminded me of the time."

"Are you?" The rhetorical question was accompanied by an enigmatical smile. Steve intertwined his fingers in hers. "I'll walk you to your car."

When, minutes later, Steve Cameron had seen her safely installed behind the wheel of her red Volkswagen, he leaned down and brushed her lips in a fleeting kiss.

"This time you can believe me when I say *au revoir*, Jolie."

Then Steve retreated to the gate where the black German Shepherd sat, ears alert and his bright eyes studying the scene. Jolie raised a hand in farewell and reversed the car into the dirt lane. It was only when she had turned on to the main road that she realized Steve had not said when he would see her again. But that warm, enveloping glow in her heart radiated with his words that he would see her again. Jolie had none of the doubt of their first meeting.

As she walked into the LeBlanc house, the repercussions of her meeting with Steve Cameron, alias Etienne, began to be felt. First Mrs. LeBlanc made her inquiry as to how she had enjoyed her afternoon with Etienne. Guy stood in the doorway, his dark gaze broodingly watching Jolie's reaction. She disguised her elation with the announcement that the Temple, Steve's plantation, was Cameron Hall. Mrs. LeBlanc immediately attributed this discovery as the reason Jolie had tarried longer than she had anticipated. Jolie didn't bother to correct that assumption, excusing herself at the first opportunity to go to her room to freshen up.

"You neglected to tell us your impression of the cavalier Steve Cameron?" Guy had followed her to the staircase. Her hand gripped the banister tightly before she slowly relaxed.

"You could have told me how devastatingly handsome he is," striving for a light note so that Guy wouldn't guess the impact Steve had made. "And that Etienne and Steve were one and the same person. I thought I was meeting an elderly French gentleman."

"And were you?" he asked quietly.

"Was I what?" Jolie frowned, not following his question.

"Devastated."

Since she hadn't confided that she had met Steve previously, there was no opportunity to admit it now. So Jolie settled for a half truth of her reaction.

"I was stunned. Strangely enough I didn't even connect him at first as being the Steve you mentioned. Of course, I didn't know Etienne was Steve in French either." The way Guy was watching her mouth was disconcerting, as if he could see the kisses that had started a fire within her.

"Was I right about his experience?" he inserted when Jolie turned to continue her way up the stairs.

His prying questions irritated her and she spun around to face him. "What do you want, Guy? A blow-by-blow account of his attempt to seduce me?" Her voice trembled with barely controlled anger.

"I never dreamed for one minute that mother would send you out there to his place!" Guy muttered, his fist pummeling the wooden railing.

"Oh, come on, Guy," Jolie sighed in exasperation. "Do you really believe what I just said?"

"No, Steve's too clever to play his hand out the first time," he sneered. "But I know he was intrigued by your wholesomeness."

"I was raised on a farm. I do know a bit about the birds and bees. And after three years of college I can handle an odd pass or two

without being shattered by one measly kiss."
That may have been an outright lie but Jolie was
too angry to care.

"Then I was right—the siege has begun." His
smile was a cross between sarcasm and smug-
ness.

"But my defenses have not been breached,"
she retorted. "And they won't be!"

"Listen, Jolie." Guy's voice changed to a
pleading tone. "I'm really only trying to warn
you so you won't get hurt. I've seen Steve in action before. He just bats those big blue eyes at
a girl and smiles and she melts just like that!"
He snapped his fingers in emphasis.

"I thought that was you." Jolie didn't spare
the sarcasm.

Besides, it hurt to realize how many other
girls had been the recipient of Steve's attentions. Too much had happened today for her to
even begin to think clearly. She wished she had
never got tangled up in this conversation with
Guy. She was only becoming more confused.
Inhaling deeply, she tried to control her bat-
tered emotions.

"Look, Guy, I understand what you're trying
to say and I appreciate it. But I'm an adult and
capable of forming my own opinions and judg-
ments. I merely found Steve fascinating."

She didn't give Guy a chance to reply, turning and walking up the steps immediately. But

he was bound to have the last word. And it carried up to her.

"So is a cobra!"

THERE HAD been no attempts by Steve to contact her the following day, Friday. Jolie amost despised herself by puttering around St. Martinville with frequent stops at the LeBlanc home in the event that Steve did call. Not that she ever asked outright if he specifically had left any messages. She was much too unsure of her own attraction to him to do that. It was merely a case of being available.

But when Saturday morning dawned, most of her faith that he would contact her vanished with the dark skies of night. No matter how much she wanted to believe that the things Guy had said about him were untrue, they kept hanging about, their pinpricks of doubt deflating her bubble of happiness. Therefore when Guy suggested they spend the day together, Jolie accepted with alacrity. Luckily Guy's plans involved a group of his friends so there were no probing questions, only several rounds of tennis followed by a leisurely afternoon beside a swimming pool.

The physical exertion and subsequent relaxing warmth of the sun eased most of Jolie's tension so that when they returned to the LeBlanc home late that afternoon she was feeling quite refreshed. She hadn't bothered to change out of her red-flowered bikini, deciding instead that the long-sleeved red blouse hid the more revealing aspects of the suit. And Mrs. Le-Blanc, who had had her share of girls, didn't appear to think it was at all improper for Jolie to lounge around the sun-porch dressed that way. The whole family was in a festive mood and Jolie was included quite naturally.

Then Michelle dashed upstairs to shower and change for her date with Eugene, her teacher boyfriend. Mr. LeBlanc received a phone call. Mrs. LeBlanc went to check on dinner. And Guy went looking for a newspaper to see what shows were playing in Lafayette so that he and Jolie could select the one they wanted to attend that night. That left Jolie standing alone in the room that had minutes ago been filled with jubilant voices.

She was also the only one to see the car pull up the driveway, coming to a stop near the back door. Idle curiosity drew her to the window to see the new arrival, a girl in slim-fitting white trousers and a red T-shirt that revealed every voluptuous curve, hop out from the driver's side. A yellow flowered band drew the long masses of black hair away from her face and cascaded it down her back. The girl moved with feline grace toward the trunk of the car, her red lips moving with animated happiness although no sound carried into the house.

The color drained from Jolie's face as Steve stepped from the opposite side of the car and walked to the rear. A memory clicked in her mind. Claudine was coming home today, the same Claudine who considered Steve Cameron her private property. And there he was with her calmly unloading suitcases and packages from the trunk of her car. Feeling like a person just betrayed, Jolie watched the smiling interchange between the two as Claudine began adjusting bags and packages until Steve looked like a hotel bellhop with cases in his hands and under his arms.

Jolie was all ready to turn away from the window so that when they entered the house they would not be aware she had been watching. But the scene had not played itself out yet. She saw Claudine move to stand closer to Steve. She watched the long, artistic fingers spread themselves on his chest, pushing open the tan shirt already half unbuttoned so her hands were resting on the hair-covered skin. Steve was looking down at the girl and although Jolie couldn't see his expression, she knew he wasn't repulsed by Claudine's actions.

A sickening nausea began churning the contents of her stomach as Jolie watched the fingers curl around his neck and pull Steve's head down toward the girl. Like a fool she kept thinking he would break free from the embrace, but he accepted the kiss. Only it wasn't acceptance, because even though his arms were laden, Jolie could see he was returning it. Then she couldn't see any more for the tears that clouded her eyes.

Now she did turn away from the window, hastily wiping her eyes with the back of her hand. She wasn't about to give him the satisfaction of seeing her cry. If he could kiss without feeling then so could she! It was just as well she had witnessed that scene, Jolie told her crying heart. There was little doubt any more as to just how foolish her hopes were. Hadn't she been warned that she was nothing more than an intriguing diversion for Steve?

There was no way she was going to be the lone person in the room when Claudine and Steve walked in the door. Jolie hurried into the hallway. She immediately saw Guy in the dining room bending over the table where the newspaper was lying.

"Did you find anything good?" Jolie forced a complete contrast to what she was really feeling.

"Come and take a look. See if anything strikes your fancy."

Jolie was determinedly studying the paper when the sound of laughter and opening doors heralded the arrival of Claudine and Steve. Guy sighed as he straightened, giving Jolie a resigned look.

"The Queen Bee has finally arrived at the hive." He very reluctantly took Jolie's hand and led her toward the hallway.

If Guy's lack of enthusiasm was noticeable, his parents more than made up for it as they affectionately welcomed their daughter home. Jolie and Guy were standing behind the group. She was grateful for these extra few minutes before she had to meet Steve face to face. The instant Guy had seen Steve with Claudine, his hand had tightened his hold on Jolie's and drawn her closer to him, a situation she was quite satisfied to have occur.

Jolie was sure they had made no sound to draw attention to themselves. Yet, with sort of a sixth sense, Steve turned from the adulation being heaped on Claudine to look behind him. His face seemed devoid of any expression, although there seemed to be a hint of amusement lurking in the depths of his cobalt blue eyes as his gaze flicked over Jolie's hand held so firmly by Guy. A betraying flush of color crept up her neck, but she boldly returned his glance, daring him to comment. If Steve saw the challenge in her eyes, he ignored it, choosing instead to let his gaze roam over her scanty attire until she felt she was nearly naked.

Before Jolie had an opportunity to exhibit her annoyance at the way Steve's gaze was taking liberties, Emile LeBlanc greeted him in French. His retort was also in French, which continued for several exchanges in the same language. Not once did Steve hesitate for a correct word, proving himself as fluent as the LeBlancs. Jolie grudgingly admired his ability and understood why Mrs. LeBlanc had referred to him by the French equivalent of his name. She refused to allow herself to wonder how he came upon the almost native ease with a foreign tongue.

"Is this your new girlfriend, Guy?"

There was a bite to the question that drew Jolie's gaze sharply from Steve to the girl now facing her. The dark, dark brown eyes were inspecting her with contemptuous thoroughness. Jolie's self-confidence was deflated by the strikingly beautiful Claudine. Here was the personification of all Jolie's dreams of the glamorous looks which she had been denied. Claudine's complexion was a flawless shade of ivory, a perfect contrast to her black hair, raven brows and long curling lashes that owed little to the artifice of cosmetics. Large gold loops hung from delicate ears, giving the girl an exotically gypsy appearance. Claudine was an orchid and Jolie felt like a field daisy standing beside her.

Vaguely she heard Guy explaining her presence as a guest, somehow omitting the fact that she was a paying one. But Guy's attempt to give importance to her status did little to boost Jolie's ego. The sheer futility of attempting to compete with anyone as beautiful as Claudine for Steve's attention was a lead weight on her heart.

That, coupled with the fact that Claudine had turned away from Jolie, dismissing her as unworthy of her attention, to direct herself to Steve, made Jolie tug at Guy's hand. He looked down on her gently and apologetically.

"I think I'll go and change," she whispered, noticing out of the corner of her eye the way Steve was listening to Claudine with intense interest.

"We'll eat out somewhere," Guy said firmly but quietly. Jolie couldn't stop the smile of relief from curving her mouth.

"Are you two going somewhere?" Claudine was suddenly interested in them now that it looked as if part of her audience was leaving.

Jolie let Guy make the explanation and escaped Steve's eyebrow that had raised in her direction.

CHAPTER EIGHT

BY THE time Guy and Jolie returned late that evening, the house was silent. There was no way of telling whether Claudine was home or out with Steve, and Jolie wasn't about to voice her speculations to Guy. After Sunday morning church, Guy arranged a jaunt with Michelle and her boyfriend for the four of them to drive down to Jean Lafitte's famous pirate stomping grounds, Grand Isle on Barateria Bay. Claudine was still in bed asleep, so there was no reason to suggest that she accompany them.

On Monday, Jolie chose to forsake the area entirely and journeyed to Baton Rouge, taking the interstate highway system that bridged the twenty miles or so of swamps in between on cranelike legs of concrete pilings. On her return to the LeBlanc home that evening, Claudine was missing from the gathering. But Jolie didn't inquire about her whereabouts. She was bound to be with Steve.

After having sleep elude her for much of the night, Jolie wakened late the next morning. She very nearly walked right back out of the kitchen when she saw Claudine seated at the table with her mother. But she had never before allowed envy for another person's looks to stand in her way and she wasn't about to be intimidated by them now. So, helping herself to a cup of coffee, Jolie joined them at the table as nonchalantly as she could.

"Good morning." She addressed her bright smile to both Claudine and Mrs. LeBlanc. The former barely glanced her way while Mrs. LeBlanc returned the greeting.

"What are your plans for today, Jolie? I was just suggesting to Claudine that she might show you around."

"There's no need for that," she replied quickly, noting the bored look on Claudine's face. "I was thinking of driving to Jefferson Island and touring the gardens there, but I feel too lazy for that today. Besides, I wouldn't want to interfere with Claudine's plans."

"I was thinking of going into the country today and doing some sketches. The watercolors of Steve's plantation sold quite well." The vague smile that flitted across the crimson lips said quite plainly that Claudine had more important things to do than act as a tour guide for Jolie. While Jolie couldn't help wondering, a little cattily, how convenient it was that Claudine's work would take her to Steve's home.

"I've seen some of your paintings. I thought they were quite beautiful." It was difficult quelling the desire to reply with a bit more coldness, but Jolie succeeded in sounding pleasant.

"Most of them are a trifle commercial." There was that saccharine smile again. "Few people see my more serious work, but then few people would understand it."

Jolie felt herself firmly placed in the plebian level of art appreciation. If she had been a dog, her hackles would have been rising about then. As it was, she sipped her coffee and smiled.

"Did I tell you, Claudine," Mrs. LeBlanc inserted with her usual exuberance, "Jolie discovered that Etienne's plantation was once owned by one of her ancestors?"

"No, you didn't. How interesting." Dark eyes turned to Jolie in slow speculation that spoke of reassessment. "How did you find that out?"

Something told Jolie that she should tread very softly in her explanation.

"One day last week, Thursday I think, Mr. Cameron," she secretly thought the formal touch was very clever, "invited me out to tour his plantation. He showed me the pillars along the bayou with the name Cameron etched on them. My ancestor's name was Cameron and they had called their plantation Cameron Hall."

"Your ancestor was an American?"

Jolie had already learned that in pre-Civil War Louisiana the landed French considered Americans as uncivilized and barbaric. Doors opened very slowly to 'Yankees' even if they were from south of the Mason-Dixon line. Therefore Claudine's question had a slightly snobbish ring to it.

"As a matter of fact, she was descended from a very old Creole French family. Her father Robert Cameron was the son of Scottish immigrants. He was killed in the Civil War, fighting for the South. A few years after the war was over, her mother remarried, this time to an officer in the Northern Army. Cameron Hall had already been sold for back taxes," Jolie concluded.

"A very interesting story," Claudine murmured languidly.

"It really is quite a coincidence that Jolie's Cameron Hall is once again owned by a Cameron, I think," Mrs. LeBlanc commented brightly.

"Personally, I wish Steve didn't own it." Her daughter ground out her cigarette in the ashtray. "He would be much better off if he didn't."

"How can you say that?" her mother exclaimed. "It's a beautiful place."

"Then let the National Trust remodel it," Claudine retorted. "Have you any idea how

ARE THESE THE KEYS TO YOUR NEW CADILLAC COUPE DE VILLE?

INSTRUCTIONS:
With a coin, scratch off the silver on your lucky keys to reveal your secret registration numbers. If they match, return this entry form—you instantly and automatically qualify to win a brand new Cadillac Coupe de Ville!

YOUR UNIQUE SWEEPSTAKES ENTRY NO.

№ 1H419102

☐ **YES,** please enter me in the Sweepstakes and tell me if I've won the $1,000,000.00 Grand Prize, or any other prize. Also send me my four *free* Harlequin Presents plus a *free* mystery gift as explained on the opposite page!

108 CIH CAN9

NAME	(PLEASE PRINT)	
ADDRESS		APT.
CITY	STATE	ZIP

☐ No, don't send me my free books or the free mystery gift, but do enter me in the Sweepstakes.

Return this card **TODAY** to qualify for
the $1,000,000.00 Grand Prize **PLUS** a
Cadillac Coupe de Ville **AND** over
5000 other cash prizes!

If offer card is missing, write to: Harlequin Reader Service® 901 Fuhrmann Blvd P.O. Box 1867 Buffalo NY 14269-1867

DETACH ALONG DOTTED LINE

much it costs to restore that broken-down mansion? Steve could be moderately wealthy if he didn't keep pouring money into that place trying to fix it up to make it partially habitable. The upkeep on such a monstrosity, even if it were like new, would be outrageous!"

"Surely he could open it up to tourists once it's restored," Jolie suggested quietly, angered by Claudine's cold practicality. "He could get back some of his costs."

"Old plantations are two for a penny in the South. The Temple, or Cameron Hall or whatever you want to call it, is hardly more unique than scores of others," Claudine answered caustically. "His plantation can't even boast of hoof prints where Union soldiers rode their horses up the stairs."

"I should think being an artist you'd want to see it restored." Jolie kept her voice steady and calm as she stirred her coffee, hoping not to show her distaste for such a mercenary attitude.

"I don't care for the cliché life of an artist. Starving in a garret never did appeal to me." Malicious amusement sparkled wickedly in Claudine's dark eyes. "A modern home or a beautiful apartment is much more comfortable than a cold and damp, partially restored plantation."

"Always, she talks like this," Mrs. LeBlanc protested with a Gallic lift of her hands to the air. "She lets her head rule her heart."

"An aspirin can cure a headache, Mama." Claudine rose from the table and carried her coffee cup to the sink. "But what is the cure for heartache?"

Jolie was curious to know the answer to that rhetorical question since she just might need the remedy herself if she didn't get Steven Cameron out of her system in a hurry. Claudine's departure from the kitchen brought a sudden bustle of activity from her mother. Jolie finished her own coffee and returned to her room, trying to work up some enthusiasm for the long day spreading before her.

SUNLIGHT FLOODED the bedroom, spraying golden beams on the sleeping figure. A bird trilled its wake-up call outside the window, causing Jolie to stir slightly, her eyelids tightening against the brilliant glare trying to penetrate her sleep. A strong floral scent teased her nose to wakefulness. She sighed, blinked her eyes and started to snuggle into her pillow for a few extra winks. But those few, barely focused blinks had seen something that shouldn't have been there.

A line creased her forehead as Jolie opened her eyes wide and stared in disbelief at the pillow beside her head. A large, full-blooming rose lay on the white case, its rich pink color contrasting sharply with the white. Very slowly she inched her hand from beneath the covers, half expecting the rose to disappear before her eyes. But when her fingers touched the stem, Jolie knew it was real. She pushed herself upright, burying her nose in the fuchsia petals.

Two things clicked simultaneously in her mind, Steve's reference to an old plantation custom of awakening guests with a rose and the feeling that she wasn't alone in the room. Her hand reached out to grab the fallen covers and pull them up to hide her skimpy cotton pyjamas even as she turned to look at the dark area near the window. The hands that had been tapping his mouth while Steve studied her with silent concentration fell to the arms of the chair as he pushed himself to his feet.

"How did you get in here?" Jolie breathed, feeling that the wind had just been knocked out of her.

"Through the door."

He leaned against the bedpost, not showing any remorse for the way he was looking at her or the embarrassing position she was in.

"You shouldn't be here! What if Mrs. Le-Blanc finds out?"

"She isn't here! I found a note downstairs for you. It seems she'll be gone all morning."

"But why are you here?" Jolie was beginning to feel a little ridiculous with the bedcovers clutched around her neck with one hand and the pink rose in the other. The blood was no longer pounding in her temples, but a trembling had taken over her limbs.

"I had the feeling you were trying to avoid me."

"That's silly." But Jolie couldn't meet his gaze.

"I'm glad to hear that." A smile spread across his face with captivating charm. "You look very desirable first thing in the morning. Did you know that? All rumpled and soft."

She blushed furiously, not knowing how to reply to such a personal comment. The velvet soft chuckle from Steve didn't help. It angered her that he should find the situation so funny.

"Now that you've determined that I'm not trying to avoid you, I think you should leave my bedroom," letting him feel a bit of her temper.

"Why? Are you afraid I'll crawl into the bed with you? I admit the idea has some merits." The blue eyes danced over her.

"You wouldn't dare!" Jolie whispered, hating the betraying leap of her heart.

Steve just smiled and reached out for her robe draped over the end of the bed. Walking to the side of the bed nearest Jolie, he stood looking down at her for an eternity of seconds before finally handing her the robe.

"I'll give you fifteen minutes to meet me in the kitchen, then I'm coming back up to get you."

While Jolie spluttered indignantly, Steve walked calmly out of the room. She was down in ten minutes, still fuming that he was so sure she would fall in with his wishes and angry with herself because she was. Yet she knew it hadn't been an idle threat by Steve that he would come back to her room to get her. She tried to console her self-respect with that.

"Well, I'm here," she announced defiantly as she entered the kitchen.

"I poured you some coffee."

His blue eyes roamed familiarly over her, admiring the blue slacks and the matching polka dot top. But Jolie kept her features frozen, refusing to let the warmth of his gaze melt her defenses. It was difficult, especially when her nerves were jumping at the slightest sound.

"Did you find any material you liked?" Steve asked when the silence threatened to last.

"Material?" Jolie forced a frown of false bewilderment on her face.

"To re-cover the sofa and chairs," he prompted.

"I'd forgotten all about it," she lied.

"Did you?" His astuteness brought a flash of color to her cheeks that quickly receded. "I thought we might do some checking together today. If you're still interested in helping?"

"Claudine would have a much better eye for material than I would." Jolie lifted her chin a trifle high as she met his gaze with all the coldness she could put into her face. "Why don't you get her to help you?"

"I asked you."

"I know," she retorted sharply and quickly before controlling the desire to resort to sarcasm. "But that was before Claudine returned."

"What you're really trying to say is that you don't trespass on other people's property, isn't it?" There was a barely perceptible smile on his face, enough for her to know that Steve was mocking her.

"Something like that," Jolie replied carefully.

"Just to set the record straight, I belong to no one. Claudine and I have known each other for a long time and we have a lot in common. But I don't run her life and she doesn't run mine. Now do you want to spend the day with me or would you rather persist with your Puritan morals and be alone?"

"Claudine seemed very fond of you and you acted as if you liked her. Naturally I assumed you were very close." Jolie sprang quickly to her own defense. "I'm not the only one who thinks that way. So do Guy and Michelle."

"I think you're reading more into Michelle's words than she means. As for Guy, he's merely protecting his flanks." The knowing gleam was in his eyes as Jolie shifted uncomfortably in her chair. Steve rose and walked around the table. "Come on, let's go."

"I haven't said I would go," she protested as he pulled her chair away from the table. Taking her arm, Steve guided her toward the back door.

"After the fool you've made of yourself, your pride probably won't allow you to give in, so I'll just bully you into accompanying me." The wide smile as he looked down at her took her breath away. "What would Guy call it? The masterful touch or the iron hand in the velvet glove?"

"He'd probably call it kidnapping," Jolie retorted, hearing the door slam behind them.

"Then I'll have you at my mercy all day," Steve chuckled, opening the door of his station wagon and helping Jolie inside.

"And will you?" she asked quietly when he slipped behind the wheel.

"Will I what?"

"Be merciful," she replied in a small voice.

Steve paused before turning the key in the ignition, regarding her with intense silence. "If you promise not to turn the force of those soft brown eyes on me. They can be very unsettling to a man's equilibrium."

Jolie turned away quickly, wondering if he knew how dangerous his deep blue pools were and how often she had wanted to drown herself in their depths. Still, it was exciting to discover that there was something about her that disturbed him. But was it a weapon or a liability, considering her own weak defenses?

When Steve turned in the direction opposite from the downtown business district of St. Martinville, Jolie glanced at him curiously.

"Where are we going?"

"New Iberia." Steve spared a glance from the road to look reassuringly at her. "I thought we'd have a bigger selection of upholstery material to choose from as well as take in some of the sights. Have you been there?"

"Just to the plantation called the Shadows on the Teche. I went yesterday," she replied, remembering how difficult it had been to enjoy the day after her conversation with Claudine in the morning.

"Did you like it?"

"Oh, yes, it was very beautiful, especially the lawns and the little gazebo along the bayou," Jolie was able to admit honestly. She had been too abstracted to take in the beautiful interior furnishing in any detail, but she had wandered the small walled lawn at her leisure, delighting in the chameleons that abounded in the shrubbery. "I did notice that the front of the house faced the street instead of Bayou Teche."

"That's because the Old Spanish Trail passed there, which prompted them to reverse the normal procedure," Steve explained. "Did you go out to Avery Island?"

"No." Jolie shook her head.

"We'll drive out there after lunch," he stated, turning his attention back to the road.

Jolie found herself settling back against the seat in contentment. It seemed natural for Steve to be behind the wheel, his strong hands firmly guiding the car. It was an extremely pleasant sensation sitting there in the seat beside him and knowing she was going to spend the entire day with him at his request. Steve would never know how important the time he spent with her was to Jolie. It was too important, considering the uncertainty of their relationship. The probability that she was nothing more than a passing fancy was too great to be ignored regardless of the depth of her own feelings.

At the second store where they stopped in New Iberia, they found the exact material that Jolie had had in mind for the sofa and chairs. It was a crushed velvet material in a very light shade of moss green, a perfect complement to the dark walnut wood. Unfortunately there wasn't sufficient material on the bolt of fabric to do all three items. The clerk assured them that he could get another shipment of the same material in the same color.

"I think we should wait until the other bolt comes in," Jolie said to Steve in a confidential tone. "It's quite possible that the material might not be the exact shade."

"I think you're right," Steve agreed, turning to the clerk to advise him of their decision.

After determining that the new shipment would arrive in less than a week, Steve escorted Jolie back to the station wagon.

Glancing at his gold wristwatch, he said, "It's still about an hour before lunchtime, but since you didn't eat any breakfast, why don't we eat now?"

"I am getting hungry," Jolie admitted.

"Do you like Mexican food? I know a good restaurant that makes some marvelous tacos."

"Sounds great."

Rafael's was a small, unpretentious restaurant located on one of the side streets. Its interior decoration was a combination of simplicity and elegance in a classical Mexican-Spanish atmosphere. They had barely seated themselves at a table when a swarthy older man entered the dining area from one of the back rooms. The moment he spied Steve, his face broke into a beaming smile as he strode to their table.

"Esteban!" was the first word uttered, followed by a torrent of Spanish that Jolie's meager high school course couldn't begin to keep up with. She was able to determine that Steve was Esteban and the man greeting him was Rafael, the owner. The familiarity and gladness of their tones convinced her that Steve was a frequent visitor to Rafael's establishment.

"Raoul, this is Miss Jolie Smith," Steve presented. "She's vacationing here in Louisiana." Turning to Jolie, he continued, "I'd like you to meet Rafael Alvarez, a very close friend of mine."

"*Buenos dias*, Señor Alvarez," extending her hand to the older man.

"Ah, do you speak Spanish, *señorita*?" The man bowed graciously over her hand.

"On the 'hello,' 'goodbye,' 'how are you' variety," Jolie admitted.

"What a pity!" Señor Alvarez smiled ruefully. "It is a beautiful language for lovers. You must have Esteban teach you." Dark eyes danced suggestively at Steve, who was regarding her with speculative amusement. "He is *mucho hombre*."

Steve staved off further personal remarks by asking Rafael what he recommended for a light lunch. Jolie didn't pay too much attention to the suggestions offered, letting Steve choose for her as she let her thoughts wander.

"You look in a daze," Steve said when Rafael left the table. "What's troubling you?"

"I was...just wondering." Jolie inhaled deeply. "You speak French fluently and now Spanish. It's not really a common thing."

"So now you're curious."

"Yes. I mean, I know that now you own a plantation, but before that...? You must have learned to speak those different languages before you ever moved here. I was wondering what kind of work you did before."

"I was an officer on a tramp ship for about eleven years," Steve replied.

"What's a tramp ship?" Mentally Jolie was picturing an old derelict ship.

"She was a very respectable vessel," Steve insisted with a bit of amusement at her doubtful expression. "It's a term applied to ships who don't have a regular port of call. They might take a load of grain from New Orleans—for example to, say, Japan and from there they might take cargo to India and so on. It might be two or three years before they ever return to the same port."

"Which was why and how you learned different languages," understanding dawning on her.

"Actually I speak four languages besides English. Italian and German as well as French and Spanish."

"You said eleven years. You must have been very young." Jolie glanced at him curiously from beneath her lashes. Steve didn't strike her as the type to be very open about his past.

"Seventeen. I was an orphan and had no close relatives. The sea seemed to offer a very romantic and adventurous occupation. At the time I lived in the North, Boston. I dreamed of running away to a South Sea island. I haunted the wharves for months before the captain of this tramp ship took pity on me and agreed to sign me aboard. He became, in a way, a father figure, being without a family himself. I sailed with him until he died nearly five years ago."

"That's when you came here?"

"I came back to the United States and finally ended up in New Orleans, where I met Claudine. Wandering had lost most of its magic, although the sea life was good to me." His eyes gleamed at her from across the table. "Do you want to hear any more about my sordid past?"

"Well, you did omit all the girls in the different ports." A teasing smile curved the corners of her mouth. "You must have left a string of broken hearts from one end of the earth to the other."

"The type of women I met...." His face hardened only momentarily before softening with cynical amusement. "I doubt if their hearts were broken. Respectable women seldom frequented the places where seamen seek their entertainment.''

"At least I was partially right when I thought of you as a buccaneer. You were once a sailor,'' Jolie smiled brightly as a waiter approached with their lunch.

"I must remember to give you my gold earring,'' Steve joked. "It would look much better on you than it ever would on me.''

"I don't know. A girl would look peculiar wearing only one earring. Maybe you'd better keep it as a souvenir,'' she laughed easily.

"Wouldn't you like a momento of our time together?'' Steve asked quietly just as Jolie started to pick up the steaming taco from her plate. The question caught her off guard.

"No,'' she replied sharply, knowing how vivid her own memory of Steve would be without a tangible reminder. She tried to laugh away her sharpness, but it sounded nervous and false. "You'd better keep it for another girl who would look good dressed as a gypsy.''

"Whatever you say,'' Steve shrugged indifferently, turning his attention to their meal.

CHAPTER NINE

"HAVE YOU read anything at all about Avery Island?" Steve asked after they had crossed the small bridge over the bayou and paid the toll.

"Not a thing."

"Being a Yankee Northerner, I don't imagine you've really noticed the flatness of the land here in southern Louisiana, have you?"

"Yes and no. I've noticed it. But do you mean did anything strike me as being strange?" Steve nodded and Jolie answered, "Then no, it didn't."

"Hills are so uncommon that they're truly a rarity. In New Orleans at the Audubon park, you'll find probably the only deliberately man-made hill in the world, called Monkey's Hill. Dirt was piled about forty feet high there in the 1930s so New Orleans children could see what a hill looked like."

"You're kidding!" Jolie laughed.

"No, it's the truth. That's why Avery Island was such a curiosity even in the early days. Its highest point is nearly a hundred and ninety-five feet above the marshes and bayous that surround it. That in itself made it unique, but it didn't make it valuable.''

"What did?'' Her attention swung away from the lush foliage on either side of the car back to the driver.

"Salt. It was first discovered in a briny spring in one of the ravines. Boiling it reduced it to a crystal form. But even in the early 1800s, it was still cheaper to get it in bulk from Europe. It wasn't until the War of 1812 when England blockaded the United States that it was recovered in any great quantity through very crude methods of boiling and evaporation. Later, the Civil War and the Union Blockade demanded that the South have its own salt resources. When they tried to deepen the spring, a deposit of rock salt was discovered running for miles at depths they weren't able to determine. It's been mined here ever since. We'll tour the salt mine first,'' Steve concluded, ignoring the sign for the Jungle Gardens to drive on past. "Of course, salt isn't complete without pepper. Avery Island is also the birthplace of tabasco sauce. It's made right here on the island as well.''

Jolie found the mine impressive and interesting. The ceilings towered sixty feet into the air supported by crystal pillars. Yet she couldn't forget that five hundred feet or so above was the surface. Therefore, despite the immensity of the mine, she was just beginning to feel claustrophobic when they started back to the surface.

"Feel better?" Steve asked when Jolie inhaled deeply once outside.

She cast him a startled glance. "How did you know?" she breathed.

"You were looking a bit pale," Steve smiled. "I'll remember that underground places are not your forte the next time."

"Next time"—those were magic words. Her determination to keep her feet on the ground fled as Jolie floated back to the car with Steve. It was only a short distance back to the turn-off leading to the Jungle Gardens and Bird City.

"Mayward Hill." Steve pointed to the mansion a few turns in the road past the entrance gate. "It's the focal point of the Gardens and the former home of the late Edward Avery McIlhenny who was responsible for the creation of the Jungle Gardens and Bird City. I hope you like to walk." A disarming smile was directed at Jolie.

"The road doesn't end here," Jolie observed as Steve pulled into one of the laybys. She could see where the narrow road continued on and even branched off into other directions.

"No, it doesn't, but to really appreciate the beauty of the place you should walk. Besides, it's the only way down to Bird City."

"I enjoy walking," Jolie asserted quickly as she scrambled out of the car to join Steve. "I only made the remark because the road continued on."

"Well, we aren't going to walk through the entire gardens," Steve smiled taking her hand. "The size of the place precludes that. There's more than two hundred and fifty acres of gardens. At different points of interest though, there are parking areas and paths to lead you back to a specific place."

The path they were on led them past giant stands of imported bamboo to culminate with a pier and lookout tower extending over a large lagoon. All types of water-fowl were present in varying numbers. The birds considered the human visitors as commonplace and ignored them while Jolie and Steve watched. It was such a serene place that Jolie was loath to leave it, but Steve convinced her that there was much more to see and they made their way back to the car.

The road twisted and turned and meandered through the grounds. Magnolia trees and giant oaks sometimes towered on each side to be replaced by lofty stands of bamboo or low, flowering hedges. Azaleas were everywhere. They stopped, walked through the sunken garden and the camellias, saw waterfalls built of old sugar kettles, then drove again with the Petite Answ Bayou on their right and the slender ribbon of a lagoon on their left. A palm-tree-lined road led to another small parking area and a sign directing them to the famous Cleveland Oak used years ago as a survey point for the original grant. This time Jolie needed no invitation to take the walking path leading back to it, stepping out of the car eagerly for a first-hand view of another section of the Gardens.

They paused beneath the giant tree, noting where nature and time had taken their mark with broken limbs and gnarled wounds carved into its moss green body. Yet the tree itself looked sturdy enough to endure hundreds of years more even with its shroud of gray Spanish moss like an aging bearded man. But the path didn't end at the Cleveland Oak, but continued on into junglelike growth.

"Where does it lead?" Jolie wondered aloud.

"Shall we find out?" The knowing look was on his face as he spread out his hand for her to precede him. "Watch your step, though. This path isn't used very much so it's bound to be overgrown and a little slippery."

In places the concrete slabs were covered with moss and in others they were chipped and broken. Steve's hand on her elbow helped her over the worst parts, although his touch by itself was unsettling. A tiny streamlike lagoon appeared and bordered one side of the path while tall bamboo canes rose on the other. At a bend in the path, two white swans came into view swimming slowly in the water. Invisible propulsion moved them with regal elegance, causing only the slightest ripple in the mirror-smooth water.

Jolie was so intent on watching the stately birds that she didn't pay attention to the uneven ground ahead of her. Her toe hit a jutting piece of concrete and she stumbled forward with the grace of an awkward duckling. But Steve's arm was there preventing her from falling in an ignominious heap. Breathless embarrassment reddened her cheeks as she stammered her thanks. She tried to slip free of the arm about her waist that held her against the warm hardness of his body, but Steve refused to loosen his hold.

Whispering softly into her hair, he said, "It was inevitable, you know. You had to end up in my arms one way or another."

Almost before Jolie could twist around to face him, his lips were clinging to hers in a possessive kiss. All the longing to be in his arms that she tried to suppress burst free as she gladly gave herself up to his embrace. His mouth all but ravaged hers while his hands explored her body, crushing her against him in the urgency of his ardor. Jolie felt herself being carried to new, dizzying heights of love and desire, surpassing the barely kindled flame of their first kiss. What had once been a glowing warmth of love became a burning, raging fire. And Steve's expert caresses knew exactly how to add more fuel.

The collar of her blouse was pushed away so his mouth could explore the hollows of her shoulder while his fingers raked the waving feathers of her hair. But her sensations were beyond registering pain, for Jolie felt the same frustrating need to explore every inch of Steve's body, too. She was reeling in a kaleidoscope world of bursting lights that sent her rocking at every new touch from him. And while she lacked Steve's experience in making love, she more than made up for it with her desire to please, which left Steve totally in control.

The laughter of children a short distance away finally stilled Steve's kisses before their lovemaking carried them further. Yet he didn't set her away from him, but kept her in the circle of his arms, her head resting against his chest until her thudding heart slowed to a less erratic pace and her breathing was less shaky. Though she still wanted his kisses, Jolie was sensible enough to realize that if it hadn't been for the sound of other people, their embrace had got to the point where she would have allowed Steve to take any liberties he wanted with her. The depth of her love for him gave him unlimited power.

Steve's hand moved to the back of her neck, letting his fingers tangle themselves in her short hair before his thumb moved forward to raise her chin. Jolie didn't make any attempt to dim the radiant lovelight in her eyes. There was no need to hide from Steve what he must already have guessed.

"You start your own fires, don't you?" he muttered hoarsely. The recently banked fires glittered with blue flames out of his eyes as his gaze roamed possessively over her face. "How have you managed to conceal this passionate side of your nature? Somebody should have snapped you up and married you a long time ago."

"The lady has to be willing," Jolie whispered, feeling herself drowning in his gaze.

There was a sharp intake of breath as Steve read between the lines of her words. His arms tightened about her briefly as his eyes darkened and narrowed. A grim smile accompanied a firm slap on her rump.

"That is for playing with fire," he scolded her with fierce gentleness. "You say that once too often and some man just might believe you."

The boldness of her words brought a pair of crimson patches to her cheeks. "I'm of age," she retorted defiantly, turning her face away from him.

Steve turned her completely around so that her back was to him, pushing her so that she was forced to continue along the path on legs that were still slightly unsteady. A supporting hand remained on her hips.

"Don't remind me," he replied as he followed her. "I'm having enough trouble trying to make sure you don't lose your self-respect, let alone mine for myself."

Jolie felt properly chastised by his words. What she had said before had only been big talk. She knew she would never be able to convince her conscience that it was all right to go to bed with a man who was other than her husband. Oh, Steve could carry her away all right, but silent recriminations would always rain down on her head from inside. It was very obvious that Steve recognized this. Which didn't leave her in an enviable position since he had stated that his freedom was very precious. Jolie pivoted around abruptly so that Steve nearly ran into her.

"I'm sorry, Steve," she blinked up at him. "You were right about what you said."

His hands were resting lightly on her hips as he stared grimly down at her. "Will you stop looking at me with those brown eyes of yours? You make it increasingly difficult to keep my hands off of you." Jolie could tell the lightness in his voice was forced. "And I don't think this is the place for a torrid love scene with the Buddha looking on."

At his peculiar remark, Jolie glanced over her shoulder. On a small hill in a glass-enclosed temple sat a large golden Buddha surrounded by his seven hills, gazing down on a small pool that cast his reflection in the late afternoon sun. She only needed a slight nudge from Steve to continue along the path that brought them closer to the base of the temple.

The Chinese Garden was a popular stop for nearly all the visitors, so that the privacy Steve and Jolie had usually had when touring a special section in this case was not to be. So, after climbing the steps to the temple and getting a closer look at the Buddha that eight hundred years ago had sat in the Shonfa Temple near Peiping, China, they walked back to the car. This time they took the more public narrow road instead of the path, eliminating the opportunity for further shared intimacies.

Under the arched wisteria vines, past the cactus gardens and the camellias, completing the loop at Mayward Hill, they drove on toward the exit gate. The sun was hovering very near the horizon, casting rich golden-orange rays that held off for a time the crimson colors of sunset. Jolie sighed deeply as they passed the stone gates. They, more than the sun, signaled the end of the day, or at least her day with Steve. It was time for him to take her home, and she wanted the day to go on forever.

"Have dinner with me tonight," Steve said in that peculiar ordering tone of his that laughed at the question form.

"I'd love to," Jolie agreed eagerly, pausing long enough to add hesitantly, "but I'm not dressed for it."

"Neither am I," he laughed, glancing down at his white polo shirt and black and white checked slacks. "But few places around here are that formal." He looked over at her provocatively. "About the only way I could imagine you looking any better would be if you were wearing nothing at all."

The heat spread from her neck all the way up her chin, suffusing her face with color. She had never realized she could be so embarrassed at the thought of her own nudity, but then it was the words being spoken from Steve's lips that were really the cause.

"I shouldn't make you blush, but you do it so beautifully." Steve reached across the seat with his free hand and took hold of hers. "Where would you like to go for dinner? That's a nice safe subject."

"I don't know anything about the restaurants around here," she replied, liking the warm, firm grip of his hand. It made her feel she belonged to him.

"Do you like seafood?"

"I haven't eaten any except shrimp and lobster back home."

"That settles it." As he shook his head at her in mock pity. "Seafood it shall be."

The picturesque restaurant sat next to a bayou, supported by stilts that raised it three feet above the ground. The outer walkway resembled a pier complete with nets draped over the railing and hurricane lamps hanging on the weathered exterior of the building. Inside, paintings of sailing ships in heavy seas and quiet harbor scenes adorned the walls side by side with mounted trophies of swordfish and others of the gamefish species. The dark-paneled walls were illuminated by sconces of modern-style chimney lamps and matching chandeliers hung from the beamed ceiling. The simplicity of life at sea was expressed in the common oilcoths that covered the tabletops, evoking an atmosphere of informality.

Steve excused himself to make a phone call as soon as they had been seated at a table. Jolie studied the menu intently until he returned a few minutes later. He hadn't mentioned who he was calling and Jolie didn't want to appear nosy by asking. The question must have been in her expression when she glanced up at him from behind her menu.

"I called the LeBlancs so they wouldn't be expecting you for dinner tonight," Steve smiled, picking up his own menu and opening it.

"I should have thought of that. I didn't leave a note or anything to tell them where I'd gone," she sighed ruefully. "I hope I didn't put them out."

"They said it was fine. What have you decided to have tonight?" adeptly changing the subject as he saw the waitress glancing in their direction.

"I can't make up my mind whether to have something safe like shrimp that I know I like, or to experiment with something new that I might not like. Maybe I could go half way. What does boiled shrimp taste like?"

"Try the seafood platter," Steve suggested, his understanding smile laced with amusement. "It has a little bit of everything. If you're adventurous enough?"

Jolie agreed, only to doubt her decision later when the heaped plate arrived and she didn't see anything on there that she recognized except french-fried shrimp. One particularly repulsive item had a round body with legs sticking out from it in all directions. For some reason, the only thing she could liken it to was a giant spider, which did little to settle the queasy feeling in her stomach. Steve had ordered the same thing for himself and was quick to notice Jolie's look of confused doubt.

"These are fried oysters." He indicated three scrunched-up pieces that were crispy brown. Pointing to two small rounded items, he said, "This is stuffed shrimp and the other is stuffed crab. Over here is the boiled shrimp which looks quite like the shrimp used in cocktails. Usually it's served still in its shell-like covering. Naturally we have fried shrimp and also some catfish, here I believe." His fork finally stopped at the last item on the platter, the one that first caught Jolie's eyes. "And this is a soft-shelled crab."

Jolie started out with the familar fried shrimp, graduating slowly to the oysters that didn't taste at all like their slimy cousins in oyster stew. The stuffed shrimp and crab were delicious. And the boiled shrimp had a delicate seasoning that was pleasantly spicy. The catfish was not any different from what she had eaten in South Dakota. The only thing left she hadn't tasted was the soft-shelled crab. She forked a small portion out of the soft belly and raised it hesitantly to her mouth. It took her a minute to forget its source and admit that it tasted good. The second bite was better than the first. She was beginning to feel quite proud of herself until Steve spoke.

"On a soft-shelled crab, you eat the legs and all."

"You're joking!" Jolie stared at him incredulously, then looked down at her plate and added silently, "Not this girl!"

"I'm not." Steve's attempt to hide his amusement was not very successful. "You really do eat them."

To prove his point, he pulled one of the larger legs off the crab on his plate and popped it into his mouth. Jolie's eyes nearly popped out of her head as she watched him chew it up and swallow. An abrupt laugh came out of her opened mouth when she realized it wasn't a trick and the crab leg wasn't going to reappear by magic.

"Honestly, they're very good. I wouldn't tease you. Try one," he urged.

This was not the time for her adventurous palate to desert her, especially with Steve looking on. Gathering all her courage, Jolie tore off one of the smaller legs and raised it timidly to her mouth. Before she could have second thoughts, she bit into it. Like everything else, it, too, was good.

"Actually the larger ones, the pincers, are better," Steve smiled, and returned his gaze to his own plate.

There was very little left on Jolie's platter when the waitress removed it to serve their dessert. Steve had thoughtfully ordered fresh fruit cocktail. Jolie didn't think she could have eaten anything heavier. The cocktail proved to be another surprise as the tastes of the different fruits didn't run together. The watermelon balls didn't taste like canteloupe; the pineapple didn't have the tang of the grapefruit sections; and the strawberries tasted like strawberries. At last she leaned back in her chair, comfortably full.

"That was all delicious," Jolie sighed as she watched Steve light a cigarette.

"I'm glad you liked it. It's good to eat with a woman who doesn't pick at her food."

"You don't need to remind me of how much I eat," Jolie admonished laughingly. "I guess that's what comes of being raised on a farm." She sobered slightly. "Speaking of farms, today you seemed to know what all the different kinds of plants were."

"Yes?" Steve prompted when she hesitated.

"You spent so much time at sea. I was just wondering how you were able to know so much about plants and growing things, like sugar cane and all on your plantation?"

"It didn't take many long days at sea before I discovered reading," he smiled indulgently. "Maybe it was because there was so much of the time when you couldn't see any sign of land that I became fascinated with agriculture, horticulture and geology. Anything connected with the earth interested me. So when I made the decision to buy the plantation, it was a matter of applying what I had taught myself and using common sense. Add a bit of trial and error and here I stand."

"Farming is hard work."

"Don't you think I'm capable of hard work?" Steve laughed.

"I was just remembering the first time I met you and you were telling me what a great follower of the carefree Cajun philosophy you were," Jolie smiled impishly.

"It has its merits. Life can be taken too seriously. Finding the happy medium can be difficult. I do admire their sense of humor and acceptance of things they can't change."

"You forgot their imagination," she added. "Like the legend of the crawfish."

"They have other fanciful tales, equally romantic," Steve nodded. "For instance, there's a story that when Marie Antoinette died on the guillotine, her son and heir to the throne, the Dauphin, was smuggled out of France by Royalist Louisianans. He ultimately lived here and became one of the United States' more famous persons."

"Jean LaFitte, I suppose," she guessed.

"No, John James Audubon, the famous painter of birds."

"Oh," Jolie gasped. "Wasn't he an adopted child?"

"History tells us he was born out of wedlock, although his natural father adopted him legally. But the Acadians would say it was a story fabricated to protect the Dauphin from reprisals of the Revolutionists." Steve tapped the ash off his cigarette. "They would have you believe that the records of Audubon's existence before the Dauphin's disappearance were an elaborate foil to keep his true identity from being known."

"It's kind of exciting, isn't it?" Her fingers trailed around the rim of her coffee cup. "I mean, if it were true?"

"What are you thinking about now?" Steve asked when a silence stretched across the table and Jolie continued staring at her cup.

"Lagniappe." There was a touch of wistfulness in the smile she gave to him. "That's the kind of day it's been for me. Something extra."

"And your escort, was he something extra, too?" She could barely distinguish his features through the haze of cigarette smoke.

"That barbarian!" Jolie teased. "I guess you could call him that."

Steve chuckled and ground his cigarette out in the ashtray before letting the fire in his gaze glitter across the table to her.

"You can be glad we're in a restaurant and there's a table between us."

The mock threat was accented by the sensuous curve of his mouth, sending her heart racing at the thought of Steve raining kisses of punishment on her. His hand reached out to still her fingers that were playing with her empty coffee cup. In the gentle grasp that was at the same time rough and caressing, she felt the voltage of his nearness shoot through her like electricity, relighting the safely banked glow of desire.

"Have I told you today how very beautiful you are?"

"Freckles and all?" she asked with a shaky laugh. She was too used to regarding herself as only mildly attractive not to jest at such a remark.

"I've seen many beautiful women with freckles, Jolie. And I won't let you slide out of a compliment that I meant very sincerely," Steve scolded her gently in his husky, caressing voice that sent tremors up her spine. "If anything, I envy the sun for planting so many kisses on your face so that you'll always shine so radiantly."

"You make it hard for a girl to keep her head out of the clouds," shaking her head to free herself of his enveloping spell.

"Turnabout is fair play." He gently withdrew his hand and signaled for the waitress to bring their check.

"What do you mean?"

"I'm generally the one left with the task of fighting the fires you start, as if you didn't know." His knowing gaze raked her thoroughly, leaving her in no doubt of exactly what he meant.

CHAPTER TEN

IT WAS pitch black outside when they began their drive home. There was only a sprinkling of stars in the sky and the moon was nowhere in view, although Jolie knew it must be out there somewhere. Wispy fragments of fog lay in gray clouds along the ditches near the road, occasionally sending out gossamer veils that swirled away from passing cars in a dancing mist. To Jolie, the light fog was a part of the ethereal enchantment of the moment as she sat there beside Steve.

Much too soon, Steve stopped the car at the curb in front of the LeBlanc home. Neither spoke as he turned off the ignition. Jolie wasn't in a hurry to go in and Steve wasn't prompting her to leave. He lit a cigarette, the matchlight throwing the carved features of his face into sharp relief. The silence continued to stretch out until the crickets chirping outside sounded unreasonably loud to Jolie's sensitive ears. She shifted uncomfortably in her seat and glanced over at Steve's darkened profile.

"Damn it!" he muttered savagely under his breath. With a vicious movement, he flicked the cigarette out of the opened car window before turning to face Jolie.

"What's the matter?" she whispered, wondering what she had done to make him so angry.

"You." His hand closed around the back of her neck in a painful grip. "I've never—"

She never heard what he was going to say because his mouth closed over hers. She would have moved into his arms, but his hand was firmly pinning her against the seat so she could get no closer to him. His kiss was so devastatingly sweet and possessive that the blood roared in her ears until she could hear nothing but the pounding of her own heart. Then Steve dragged his mouth away to nuzzle her neck and ear.

"I don't want you to go in," he muttered thickly in her hair.

"I don't want to either," she answered, her voice shaking with the emotion he had aroused.

Her admission served as a brake, halting his caress as he inhaled deeply and moved to his own side of the seat. He stared at her through the dimness of the car.

"You don't know what you're saying. You'd better go in.... Now," Steve added with growly emphasis. He raked his fingers through his raven black hair. "I'll ... I'll call you tomorrow."

She opened the car door, the interior light switching on automatically. Glancing over at him before swinging her legs out, Jolie saw the hunger in his eyes as they watched her. She very nearly closed the door again to move into his arms, but discretion and common sense took over and she slid out of the car. She hurried toward the house before her resolve could weaken. Once there, she opened the front door and stood in its shadow to watch Steve drive away.

The house was quiet. Only the muted sound of instrumental music on the record player in the family room indicated anyone else was there. Jolie didn't feel like facing any of the family and recounting the events of the day. She wanted to savor those moments to herself for a little while longer. So she tiptoed up the stairs to her room. Leaving her door open, she crossed her room to switch on the floor lamp. As she turned to go back and shut the door, she saw Claudine standing in the doorway.

Her brunette hair was loose and lying around her shoulders like a black cloud, contrasting perfectly with her milky-white complexion. She was wearing a robe of an exotic blue-green design that reminded Jolie of peacock feathers. Beneath the lined robe was a matching short nightgown. Even from where Jolie was standing she could see that the wispy material peeping through the top of the robe was blatantly transparent. If it wasn't for the fact that the robe was lined, Claudine would have appeared indecently clothed.

"So you're back." A dark brow was arched at Jolie. "Did you enjoy your little outing with Steve?"

"I had a very good time," Jolie replied calmly, refusing to pick up the invisible glove Claudine had thrown.

"I suppose you dragged him around to all those tourist places?"

"As a matter of fact, Steve thought I might enjoy Avery Island. So, at his suggestion, we went there."

"He's been there so many times, it's a miracle he wasn't bored to death." Claudine studied her fingernails. It was such a feline gesture that Jolie half expected to hear a miaow when Claudine looked up.

"I don't think Steve was bored," she replied with a secret smile on her face that lit a fire of anger in Claudine's dark eyes. Jolie turned away to pick up her brush and began brushing her hair. She hoped, futilely, that Claudine would take the hint and discontinue the conversation.

"I hope you don't take his attentions seriously," Claudine drawled from just behind her. "An inexperienced girl like you could get hurt."

"I think I'm old enough to take care of myself." The brush didn't skip a stroke.

"His masculinity can be overpowering. Older women than you have fallen in the wake of it."

"Including you?" Jolie blinked innocently at Claudine over her shoulder.

"I have more experience and endurance than most. I stay clear of the undertow. But I think you're out of your depth."

"That's my problem, isn't it?" Sarcasm gleamed in her eyes and the false smile on Jolie's mouth.

"Of course," Claudine retorted sharply, contorting her mouth into some semblance of a smile. "I was just trying to give you a little friendly advice. If all you have in mind is a little harmless flirtation while you're on your holiday, then have it. You won't find a better partner than Steve. But he isn't about to be tied down."

"That must be very frustrating for you." Jolie never realized it could be so much fun getting in her little digs at this paragon of a malicious friend. In fact, she was beginning to enjoy their little talk.

"Steve is a man. With a man's appetites." Smouldering rage burned in Claudine's face. "I can satisfy his needs."

"Any woman can satisfy those needs," Jolie replied calmly.

"Let's get this straight." The mask was removed now and her hate for Jolie was firmly revealed. "Right now, your innocence amuses him, but it won't last for long. He'll either seduce you, in which case your innocence will be gone, or he'll grow tired of trying and drop you. You're only a passing fancy and you might as well realize it."

"You may very well be right." It was Jolie's turn to unsheath her claws. "On the other hand, he may be getting tired of 'used' merchandise and would prefer to try something brand new so he can mold it to fit his needs."

Claudine's hand raised threateningly in the air. For a moment Jolie thought she was going to strike her. Instead Claudine turned on her heel and walked to the door. But she didn't leave. She turned, tossing her hair over her shoulder in a defiant gesture and studied Jolie contemptuously.

"You're making a very big mistake," she said icily.

"'Sticks and stones may break my bones,'" Jolie chanted quietly. She didn't have to finish it as Claudine swirled out of the room.

Well, Jolie thought to herself, *I won the first battle, but now it's war.* Claudine had been the one to drag it out in the open and it just wasn't in Jolie to back down from anyone. Regardless of what the morrow brought, it had been a satisfying day. And tonight she didn't want to worry about what might happen tomorrow. All she wanted to remember when her head rested on the pillow was the rapturous happiness she had felt in Steve's arms. She wasn't going to let Claudine's spiteful and jealous tongue disturb her dreams.

Jolie was up early the next morning donning her freshly laundered sundress, courtesy of the ever thoughtful Mrs. LeBlanc, of bright oranges and yellow flowers against a background of snowy white. She chose her dressier open-toed white sandals and took special pains applying the light make-up. When she was all done, Jolie, who was usually very critical of her own appearance, couldn't find much fault with her reflection.

Softly humming a gay tune, she skipped lightly down the steps to the kitchen. All Steve had said was that he would call her today. He had made no mention of any plans to go somewhere or, for that matter, what time he would call, morning, noon or night. But Jolie was ready for anything.

Mrs. LeBlanc, Michelle and Guy were seated around the dinette table. Emile LeBlanc had already left and Claudine had not yet risen, which didn't upset Jolie a bit. As always Mrs. LeBlanc was her cheerful self and Jolie's own bubbling happiness matched her bright greeting. Guy's brief nod in her direction was grim and condemning. But she shrugged it off easily as she poured herself a cup of coffee and seated herself in the vacant chair at the end of the table.

"You slipped off to bed last night before you gave us an account of your adventure yesterday." Michelle's eyes twinkled with a pert gleam from Jolie to her brother.

"Yes, Jolie, tell us where Etienne took you," Mrs. LeBlanc prompted, while Guy continued staring morosely into his cup.

"We went to Avery Island." Then she went on to give them some of her impressions of what she saw, carefully avoiding too much emphasis on her companion.

"Oh, you should see the Gardens in March when the azaleas and the camellias are both in bloom!" Mrs. LeBlanc exclaimed with an expressive wave of her hand. "So many colors! So many flowers everywhere! Everything is so plentiful that it seems almost pagan!"

"The best part about the Jungle Gardens, though, is that the flowers don't have to be in bloom for a person to enjoy the beauty of the place. Of course, there are different flowers blooming all year through," Jolie remarked. "I wouldn't have missed seeing it for anything."

"I'm glad Etienne took you there," the older woman smiled.

"Claudine isn't," said Guy, breaking his self-imposed silence.

"Now why should Claudine mind?" With her arms akimbo, Mrs. LeBlanc looked curiously at her son.

"Oh, Mother, surely you don't need to ask." Guy shook his head hopelessly.

"If you're trying to say that there's something serious between Etienne and Claudine, then you're wrong," Mrs. LeBlanc stated emphatically. "How long have they known each other? Four years? Five years? That's a very long time in which to find out if they're serious or not. Too long with a pair as hot-blooded as Etienne and Claudine. No, they're good friends, but nothing more."

"Mama, you're very old-fashioned," Guy smiled at her sadly.

"Maybe," she nodded. "But when a man puts a ring on a woman's finger, then you know he's serious. Before that he is only fooling around. I think you're upset because it was Jolie who was with Etienne and not because it was your sister's boyfriend who was with Jolie. You regret that it was not yourself who spent the day with her."

Guy glanced at the uncomfortable look on Jolie's face and shrugged. "You're probably right about that, Mama."

It was obvious that Mrs. LeBlanc was prepared to pursue the subject, but luckily the phone in the hallway rang, causing Jolie's heart to skip a beat in anticipation.

"I'll get it." Guy rose from the table before either his sister or his mother had time to react to the sound.

Jolie couldn't blame him for wanting to escape from the conversation, which although it was slightly embarrassing, was also very enlightening. Michelle glanced up at the clock above the kitchen sink and sighed.

"I almost wish it were the principal calling to say the water main has broken and the school is flooded. I don't feel up to facing those kids today." Even as she spoke Michelle was gathering her papers together. "I honestly think teachers look forward to the weekends more than the students. We're just too outnumbered."

"Jolie, telephone!" Guy's voice rang clearly in the kitchen.

She mumbled a breathless "excuse me" before pushing herself awkwardly away from the table. Her heart was tripping away like a jackhammer as she hurried into the hall. Avoiding the condemning glare and bitterly twisted smile on Guy's face, Jolie took the telephone receiver from him.

"Hello," she answered, knowing there was only one person who could be on the other end of the line.

"Good morning," Steve replied. His husky voice managed to transmit little tremors that tingled through her. "Did you sleep well last night?"

"Like a log," she laughed nervously, wishing Guy would return to the kitchen and stop watching her.

"That's nice. I didn't sleep a wink." A wry note crept into his voice and it caught at her breath.

"I'm sorry," she said for want of a more suitable reply.

"Are you?" Steve chuckled. "That's not much of a comfort."

"I know," Jolie turned her back to Guy and twined her fingers in the coiled receiver cord.

"I called to tell you that I'm going to be tied up today," Steve went on, amusement still tinting his words. "One of the field tractors broke down yesterday. I'll probably have to go into Lafayette for parts. It might take the better part of the day and night to get it running again."

"I understand," Jolie said, trying to hide her disappointment. "I mean . . . there was nothing definitely planned anyway, and the tractor is hardly something you could have known about yesterday."

Behind her, she heard Guy's footsteps walking toward the kitchen and unwittingly sighed her relief.

"I'm disappointed, too, Jolie." There was such quiet sincerity in Steve's voice that her heart, which had slowed at the news she wouldn't see him today, set off again at breakneck speed. "So what will you do with yourself today while I'm slaving trying to get the tractor running?"

"Miss you," she replied, pertly, liking the sound of his laughter on the other end of the phone at her answer.

"Any more comments like that and I'm liable to say to hell with the tractor," he growled with mock fierceness.

"Promise?" she said boldly, then hurried on before he could take her seriously. "I take that back. After all, I am a farmer's daughter and I know that broken machinery can't wait for a rainy day."

"Thanks, ladybird. Maybe tomorrow."

"Yes, tomorrow."

After the click of his receiver, Jolie replaced the phone in its cradle, her hand remaining on it for a short time as if she could prolong the contact with Steve. Again there were footsteps in the hall, this time coming nearer instead of retreating. Fixing a smile on her face, Jolie turned. It was Guy entering the hallway. He stared at her, his brown eyes reflecting hurt and uncertainty.

"If you're free this afternoon, we could play some tennis." The words were said in a defiant manner as if it made no difference to him whether or not she accepted him.

"I'm free," Jolie answered quietly, wishing the rising compassion would stem the guilt she felt for putting that look in his eyes. But she couldn't control the fact that it was Steve she had fallen in love with and Guy was only a friend.

Guy started to reply, then halted, closing his mouth tightly and nodding as he walked to the front door. Yet neither Guy's depressive mood nor the knowledge that she wouldn't see Steve today could darken Jolie's spirits. The phone call had confirmed her hope that Steve wanted to be with her. Probably not as much as she wanted to be with him, but he had sounded sincerely sorry that he couldn't see her. That in itself had been consolation.

By late afternoon, Guy had shaken free of the sullen mood and Jolie's slight tenseness soon vanished under his carefree demeanor. After two games of tennis with Guy the victor, though not by a large margin, a small group of his friends arrived on the courts. Jolie was no longer the object of Guy's attention as he transferred his allegiance to an attractive blonde. Since Jolie was a competent tennis player, she was a welcome partner choice in mixed and matched doubles. After a particularly blistering game where both couples were equally skilled, Jolie insisted on sitting out and catching her breath. She would have preferred to call it a day and go home, but Guy lingered even when the rest made comments in the same vein. Jolie wanted to remind him that his mother undoubtedly had the evening meal ready, but was afraid she would sound like a wet blanket. She had learned early in her dating that no man wanted to be reminded that momma had supper waiting at home.

Finally the crimson blush of twilight signaled the end of the party and Guy very reluctantly escorted Jolie to the car. He had the grace to murmur an apology which she shrugged off, teasing him about his recuperative abilities.

"I borrowed a page from Steve's book," Guy replied blandly. "I heard him taunt Claudine that there was never a woman that another woman couldn't make a man forget in time."

Did Steve really believe in that? Jolie asked herself. Because if he did, then how much did she mean to him? A terrible fear wrapped cold fingers around her heart. Was she reading too much into Steve's attention? In order to believe her love returned, was she reading more into his caresses than he intended? It was frightening to remember that Steve himself had told her that marriage was not a part of his plans. He didn't even believe that love existed. If Steve discovered that she was in love with him, would he smile and tell her that she would get over it?

With the kind of life Steve had known, it was unlikely that he would have ever known a deep abiding love of any kind. Orphaned when he was a baby, spending his early manhood at sea, drifting from port to port, never having a place to call home. No wonder he had been so drawn to Cameron Hall, the plantation that had his name carved on its gates.

But did that help her? Was he in love with her? Or would another woman supplant her memory in his mind? Was she another shipboard romance for him, just another girl in a different port?

As she sat silently in the car beside Guy, Jolie felt afraid, vulnerable and very uncertain.

CHAPTER ELEVEN

WHEN STEVE called the following day, Jolie had just left the house to run into town on a personal errand. The message he left with Mrs. LeBlanc had been that he would call Jolie that night. While she regretted missing his call, Jolie still had something to look forward to even if she had a whole day to wait.

Of course, there was always the decision of what to do with the rest of the day. Sitting idle was not something that came easily to her. The minutes passed much too slowly that way. Although the thought of more sightseeing wasn't exciting, it seemed the surest way of making the evening come quicker. About the only place nearby that she hadn't been to was the Rip Van Winkle Gardens west of New Iberia.

The stately English-style gardens seemed cold after the tropical abundance of the Jungle Gardens at Avery Island, but she was minus her companion. Jolie was sure that had a great deal to do with her lack of enthusiasm. The day was extremely hot and humid, so when Jolie drove back through the town of New Iberia, she decided to stop for a cold drink. By accident or a subconscious direction, she had parked her Volkswagen on the same block the store was located where Steve had ordered the material for the sofa and chairs. Obeying an impulse that she knew was foolish, Jolie entered the store. The sales clerk who had waited on them recognized her immediately.

He explained that the shipment had just arrived that very morning and remarked how fortunate it was that Jolie had come when he was about to contact Mr. Cameron. Since it had been prepaid, he inquired if Jolie wanted to take it today. She hesitated briefly, disliking the idea that Steve might think she was being over forward picking up the material before reasoning that she was only saving him a journey to New Iberia.

It took some maneuvering to get the bulky material into her little car, but it was finally accomplished. Not until Jolie was sitting in the restaurant two stores away did she realize how long she had tarried in the store. After a few sips of lemonade she returned to her car, not wanting to be the cause for the LeBlancs' evening meal being delayed as it had been last night when she and Guy had been late.

Jolie arrived in plenty of time for dinner but too late for Steve's call. Frustrated and angry at herself for being gone so long, she was barely

able to eat anything. Did Steve think she was
playing a game? He hadn't said he would call
again. What if he didn't? All the while she was
helping Mrs. LeBlanc carry dishes to the
kitchen, Jolie was calling herself fifty kinds of
fool. She debated calling him, but the telephone can be a cold communicator. There was
only one way, she decided. She would drive out
to Cameron Hall that very night no matter how
bold and forward it looked. Besides, she had the
excellent pretext of delivering the upholstering
material.

She didn't tell Mrs. LeBlanc anything except
that she was going out and would be back later
that evening. Dusk had already given way to
nighttime when Jolie slid behind the wheel of
her car. Michelle had just driven in after returning to the school house for some paper she
had left and Jolie was forced to wait until her
car was parked and the driveway was clear.

"Are you going out?" Michelle called on her
way to the house.

"Yes," Jolie answered without explaining
further.

"The fog is a little thick. Be careful." Then
Michelle waved and entered the house.

Once Jolie left St. Martinville and began her
way through the country, Michelle's comment
on the fog turned into an understatement. It
swirled around her so thickly that her pace was

reduced to that of a blind man without a cane. Her headlights could barely reveal the ditch alongside the road, let alone illuminate the road more than a few feet ahead of her. Moisture condensed on the windscreen to add to the difficulty of seeing. It was only by instinct that she found the correct crossroads and the road that would take her to the dirt lane leading to the plantation.

Time inched by as slowly as her Volkswagen. And the more time that went by, the surer Jolie became that she had missed the turn. Her fingers ached from clenching the steering wheel so tightly. A throbbing headache had begun at the back of her neck until her eyes hurt from the strain of peering into the gray shroud that surrounded her. A sob of despair rose in her throat that she had foolishly got herself lost when a small white sign glistened near the side of the road. It was impossible to read it as the fog thickened around it. She stopped the car altogether and stepped out, leaving the motor running while she got a closer look at the sign with the flashlight from the glove compartment.

"Private Road—No Trespassing." Unwelcome words that brought a sigh of relief. By some miracle, she had made it. The plantation was a quarter of a mile farther. The only trouble was the closer she drove to the plantation and the bayou on the opposite side, the denser the fog grew. There was no chance at all that she would be able to see the iron gates of the entrance. The only alternative was for her to guess at the distance and then explore on foot, relying on her flashlight to find them.

Four steps from the car and she could barely make out its peculiar round shape. The fact that it was red helped. Taking two steps forward, Jolie inhaled deeply, knowing that the fog had closed in around the car and hidden it completely from view. She inched her way along the ditch looking for the culvert leading to the gates while she tried to rid herself of the fear that she was only going to end up getting lost in this gray-black cloud.

In the murky darkness, she nearly missed the entrance. As usual it was padlocked. The beam from the flashlight barely penetrated the fog beyond the grille-work. Hesitantly she touched the cold, damp bars, giving them a shake to see how sturdy they were. The bell hanging from the pillar didn't seem to have any resonance at all. Jolie decided only a foghorn could pierce this. Still she waited before attempting to climb the iron bars. The last thing she wanted to have happen was for her to meet the black German Shepherd in this weather. But not even the dog appeared to welcome her.

The gate was very easy to climb over, especially for a former tomboy. On the other side, the trees and shrubs loomed ominously on either side of the narrow lane. Any moment she expected the dog to spring from the darkness, white fangs flashing in the night. The only thing her light picked out was the branches of the giant oaks, the Spanish moss taking on ghostly decoration. Jolie couldn't help thinking it was a perfect setting for one of those spooky Gothic novels. A small patch of light winked dimly at her from the garçonnière, and her already jangled nerves were set on edge when a low, rumbling bark sounded from the narrow gallery. Jolie was close enough to make out the light shining from the screen door and the dog standing guard in front of it.

"Steve!" she called out. The dog growled in answer although he didn't come any closer to her. Jolie called again, her voice sounding strange in the ghostly silence. If he were inside the garçonnière, he would have surely heard her.

The dog obviously considered her no threat since he raised no objection when she stepped onto the porch. Still Jolie hesitated to walk past the dog to the door.

"Where's your master, Black?" she asked the dog.

His tail wagged in what seemed a friendly manner and Jolie took a courageous step toward the door. Instantly the dog's lip curled and a threatening growl came from his throat. When she halted, his tail wagged again. Evidently he had decided she could be on the gallery, but the garçonnière was forbidden. She wasn't going to argue with him.

"Is it all right if I wait here for Steve?" It was silly asking the dog since he couldn't reply, but the silence of the fog was beginning to wear on her nerves. The sound of her own voice was a small comfort and at least she wasn't talking to herself.

The muggy dampness had begun to penetrate her clothing, sending its cool fingers into her bones. She shivered and rubbed her arms briskly while she glanced apprehensively around. There was no sign of Steve at all. The thought of finding her way back to the Volkswagen and then back to the LeBlanc home in this fog was frightening.

"What are you doing here?" Steve materialized catlike at the far end of the narrow gallery.

"I came to see you." Her tongue was jumping about like her heart. "I'd just decided that you weren't here."

As Steve walked closer, Jolie could see the anger dancing in his eyes. She had expected surprise, even gladness, but she hadn't thought he would be angry.

"The material for the sofa and chairs arrived today. I was in New Iberia and happened to stop." She felt compelled to fill the uneasy silence made more uncomfortable by his measuring gaze. "I left the material out in the car. I didn't have anything special to do tonight, so I thought I'd bring it out."

"How did you get here?" he demanded.

"I drove," she answered weakly under his glowering look. "I didn't realize the fog was so bad until I got out in the country." She shivered again, but not just from coldness. "I was practically here by then or I would have turned around. The dampness sure goes right through you."

"Why didn't you go into the house where it's warm?" he growled, flinging open the screen door and pushing her inside.

"According to your dog, I wasn't allowed any farther than the porch," Jolie retaliated, hurt by Steve's strange behavior.

Steve glanced at the dog sitting outside as if he had forgotten it was there. He raked his fingers through his black hair that had begun to curl slightly from the dampness.

"Sit by the fire and warm up while I get the pickup," he ordered sharply, gesturing toward the fireplace and the tiny flame licking at a solitary log. "It has foglights and I can drive your car back in the morning."

"Thanks for being so overjoyed to see me!" Jolie tossed sarcastically after him as he started for the door. There was a betraying trembling in her chin as the tears burned the back of her eyes.

"What's that supposed to mean?" Steve glared at her.

"Good grief! I drive all the way out here and I don't even get a hello, how are you before you're bundling me up and taking me home!" She had to shout or she would cry.

"How are you! How are you! You crazy, mixed-up little idiot!"

With a quaking body, Jolie watched Steve inhale deeply to control his anger. He studied her silently with his hands on his hips.

"I don't understand?" she murmured, finding it harder and harder to meet his accusing eyes.

"That's obvious," he replied grimly. "How many cars did you pass on the way here?"

"None." Jolie felt herself growing smaller.

"That's because anyone with an ounce of sense wouldn't be out in this fog."

"Michelle had just come home when I left. She didn't seem concerned."

"You didn't tell her where you were going either, did you?" Steve asked and sighed in exasperation when Jolie shook her head that she hadn't. "If you had, I'm sure she would have warned you."

"Well, she didn't, and I'm here! And you needn't be so beastly about it!" She had to cover her mouth to keep that little choking sob from making itself heard.

"You could have run off the road upside down into a ditch or been crunched like an accordion against a telephone pole!" A short angry laugh followed his outburst as he shook his head. "And I'm not supposed to be in the least upset by such thoughts. What do you think I am?"

"I didn't think you cared," Jolie whispered.

Steve covered the distance between them in one liquid movement. His fingers dug into the bones of her arms as he lifted her up onto her tiptoes.

"Cared?" he groaned. His words were muffled by her brown hair.

"You're hurting me," she protested weakly. His nearness was already dulling her senses of pain where his fingers dug into her flesh.

"You deserve it," he replied grimly, relaxing his hold enough to reduce the pressure and still retain the grip. "You can be glad that I can't make up my mind whether to turn you over my knee or to take you in my arms."

"If you feel that way," Jolie gazed into his face, thrilling to the fires she saw burning there, "then why do you want me to leave?"

"Would you rather stay here until the fog lifts? It would be tommorrow morning before it burns off. You can't honestly expect to stay all night with me without something happening, can you?''

"No, no, of course not," Jolie murmured, pulling gently away from him. "It's just that...I haven't seen you for—for so long." She felt his hands settle on her shoulders, but not so fiercely this time. "I missed your call this morning...and...and again this afternoon." She spun quickly around to face him, the longing for him revealed openly in her eyes. "I just wanted to see you."

"I wanted to see you, too." Was it her imagination or were his hands trembling as he held her? "But not here!"

"What difference does it make?"

"If I have to explain to you," Steve breathed in angrily, "then you're more innocent than I thought."

"Damn these freckles and damn my face!" Jolie cried, flinging herself away from him in a fit of temper. She looked around her desperately for something to throw to relieve her tension and found nothing. "Why does everyone keep harping on my virtuous nature? Damn my virtue! I don't feel in the least bit virtuous!"

"You don't know what you're talking about!" Steve shouted back.

"What, are you a Boy Scout all of a sudden?" she asked sarcastically, before quicksilver tears sprang from her eyes. "I can't help the way I feel about you. Don't you see? I just want you to hold me in your arms. I can't help it.''

"You're talking nonsense, Jolie."

"I'm talking to a brick wall, that's what I'm doing," she sniffled, wiping the tears of self-pity away from her face and regaining her control.

Before she had an opportunity to apologize for her unwarranted outburst, she was yanked into his arms. Her breath was knocked away as she came to an abrupt halt against his hard chest.

"I wish I were a brick wall," Steve hissed before covering her mouth with a rough, bruising kiss.

All the checked desire burst forth with the fury of a volcanic explosion as Steve ravaged her mouth, her neck and her face. In the stranglehold of his embrace, Jolie was powerless. She could neither respond nor protest as he brutally forced her to submit to his punishing kisses.

Then he was sweeping her off her feet and lifting her bodily into his arms. The crushing grip about her shoulders prevented her from seeing where he was carrying her. Her head was pushed way back as his mouth continued violating hers while her hands pushed ineffectually against his chest. His stride changed and it took Jolie a moment to realize that he was climbing the stairs. With a great surge of strength she pushed him away from her.

"Where are you taking me?" she asked, gasping for the breath he had denied her.

"The couch is too small and the floor is cold." His blue eyes gleamed wickedly into her face, their callousness frightening her more than his wrathful kisses. "My bed will be less restrictive and softer."

"No," she whimpered as he twisted her head around for his kiss, not pausing in his flight up the steps. "Steve, no!"

The savagery of his touch abated with her weak appeal without lessening the strength of his hold. Steve had stopped and was setting her back on her feet. The soft light from the stairs barely illuminated the room they were in, but there was sufficient light for Jolie to see the shining headboard of the brass bed.

"What's the matter?" Steve whispered huskily into her ear as his hands continued their rough fondling of her shoulders and back. "Don't you want me to make love to you, Jolie?"

An icy-cold numbness spread over her. "Not this way, Steve," she sobbed. "Not this way, please."

"What way is that?"

"Without any... any tenderness or... or affection," she stammered. "As if... if I... I were just any w-woman."

The humiliation in her voice brought Steve's head away from his exploration of her neck as he tilted his head upward toward the ceiling before bringing it slowly back to focus on her tear-stained face that was staring at the floor.

"I want you, Jolie," he sighed softly, his knuckles tracing the outline of her cheek. "I won't deny it."

"Why?" she persisted, needing to know the truth—the depth of his attraction to her.

"Because you're a woman and I'm a man. Is there ever any more to it than that?"

"Yes, Steve, there is," Jolie answered slowly and firmly, lifting her head up to look into his masked expression. Her own undying love for him proved that.

"You say that because you're young." There was a faraway smile twisting his mouth. "You haven't had a chance to discover how fickle humans are."

"Are you fickle? Will you forget me?"

"Maybe not completely." The way he was looking at her was as if he were implanting her image on his mind. "You're a special person. Natural, honest and giving."

"I suppose I should thank you for that compliment." There was a bitter taste in her mouth that tainted her quietly spoken words.

"I never really meant to hurt you, Jolie. I'm sorry," Steve shook his head, his hand tightening momentarily on her shoulder before he released her completely. "I'll take you home now."

"Don't be sorry for me, Steve." A flash of fire flared in her brown eyes. "My Aunt Brigitte told me once that real love was rare. Few people ever find it because most are too selfish. They are incapable of giving of themselves in more than a superficial way."

"And you think I'm one of them?" he asked coldly.

No, Jolie admitted to herself, she didn't think he was, although everything he said and did indicated it. Confusion was written on her face.

"Tell me why did you treat me the way you did just now—as if I was a common tramp or something?" she asked, unaware of the pleading tone in her voice.

"The truth?" His eyebrow arched arrogantly at her. "Because you were so naively asking for it."

"I was not!" Jolie cried indignantly. She would have raised her hand to strike him, but Steve had firmly pinioned her wrists to prevent such an attack.

"Not consciously, no. But if I'd been tender and loving as you said you wanted, we would have been in that bed right now."

"If you believe that, then why didn't you take advantage of me?" Jolie demanded, her breath coming in short angry gasps.

"Advantage. What an old-fashioned word!" he chuckled cynically. His dark blue eyes were nearly stripping her of her pride. "But, in answer to your question, I haven't sunk so low as to be seducing virgins."

"I don't understand you." She shook her head in bewilderment. "One minute you act as if you really care for me and the next you're trying to prove how cold and unfeeling you are."

His lips compressed into a grim line as he stared at her without answering. The narrowing of his eyes made Jolie aware once again of the length and thickness of his lashes. For a moment she stared hypnotically into the depths of his gaze.

"This isn't the time or the place for the kind of discussion you want," Steve said, moving past her and walking down the steps. Halfway down, he turned to look up at her. "Come on, I'll take you home."

Jolie hesitated. Another thought had just occurred to her. "Steve," she called in a fearful voice, "are you using me to forget . . . to forget Claudine?"

"What put that thought in your head?" he scowled.

"I heard...." Then she paused, knowing any reference to Guy would bring a derisive response. "I heard that men sometimes see other women in order to forget one special woman."

"Am I going to have to carry you down the stairs as well?" he asked with ominous quietness.

"Is it true ... that you ... that men do that?" she persisted, walking to the head of the stairs to look fully into his cold face.

"Yes, it's true, and quite effective. It doesn't happen to apply in this case, although the reverse might be worth considering."

"Do you mean you want to forget me?" Jolie breathed, a flicker of hope lighting her eyes.

"Especially when you test my patience as you're doing right now. For the last time, I'm taking you home. Now get down here."

Steve appeared to be encompassed by a strange brooding mood. The savagery of those earlier moments was too easily remembered for Jolie to persist in further conversation when he was making it plain that he wanted none of it. His feelings toward her were so ambivalent that she wondered if even he knew how he felt. She certainly didn't. If anything she had become more uncertain. He was too complex for her limited experience to fathom. And Jolie was sure he knew that, too.

The foglights on the pick-up truck effectively increased the visibility. Although their speed was slower than normal, it was still faster than the snail's pace Jolie had driven on the way out. For all the attention Steve paid her, she could have been an inanimate object on the seat beside him. When they pulled up in front of the LeBlanc house, Steve left the motor running, letting her know there would be no prolonged good nights.

"I'll bring your car back in the morning, probably before you're up." His harsh words revealed his hurry and Jolie reached for the door latch, but a hand on her arm forestalled her. "I have to go to New Orleans tomorrow on some business. I'll be gone a couple of days."

"Why are you telling me?" Jolie knew her question had a belligerent tone, but Steve's coldness had hurt and she wanted to strike back.

"I don't know." Steve emitted an angry sigh and reached across her to open the door. "Good night, Jolie."

CHAPTER TWELVE

"WHERE HAVE you been?"

Jolie had raced all the way into the house and was halfway up the stairs when Claudine's demanding question brought her up short. All Jolie wanted was the seclusion of her room where she could shed some of the tears that were scorching her eyes.

"On an errand, if it's any of your business," she retorted.

"It must have been a convenient errand since it enabled you to have Steve bring you back," Claudine jeered. When Jolie would have continued her flight up the stairs, the raven-haired girl went on, her dark eyes flashing like burning coals, "It's a pity you didn't invite him in. There was something I wanted to talk to him about, but I suppose it will just have to wait until tomorrow."

"It will have to wait longer than that." Jolie made her voice sound as quietly sarcastic as Claudine's, although she didn't trust herself to meet the older woman's gaze. "Steve is going to

New Orleans tomorrow. He'll be gone for a couple of days.''

"How fortunate for you!" Claudine called after her as Jolie scurried up the stairs, the soft complacency in that voice hurting more than the previous sneering words.

The little red Volkswagen was parked in its former place behind the house the next morning when Jolie arose. She had slept fitfully and the effects were revealed in the drawn look about her face and the dark circles under her eyes. She had tried hard to make herself see how illogical she had been, but there was no room in her heart for logic, only Steve. What did it matter that she had known him less than two weeks? People had fallen in love before in a matter of hours, which never made their love any less potent or lasting.

Physical attraction. Infatuation. Fascination for an older, more experienced man. All of those could be true. Jolie knew they weren't, just as she had known she didn't love John the way a woman should love her husband.

If only she could understand Steve! When she was in his embrace, Jolie was certain he desired her and maybe even more than that. Maybe he even loved her. Then with mercurial swiftness, he would declare that he didn't believe in love—that he would never marry. Was he afraid of love? It was impossible to believe that Steve was afraid of anything, and certainly not something as harmless as love.

Harmless! That was a laugh! Look at what it was doing to her. She was twisted in knots it would take an expert seaman to untangle. Seaman—that's what Steve had been. Had she thought of that analogy because Steve was the reason for her torment? The whole situation seemed so hopeless to her.

And knowing that Steve was in New Orleans made the day stretch ahead of her with incredible emptiness. Even if he were here, it might be just as discouraging. With a bit of wry humor, Jolie remembered the dilemma she had been in before she had come to Louisiana. It seemed such a petty problem now in the face of her monumental love for Steve.

Jolie knew she couldn't wander about the house all day. Mrs. LeBlanc had been very curious about her morose expression at the breakfast table. The thought of visiting any tourist spots failed to interest her. There was one thing she did want to do. It would probably be foolish and a big mistake, one that she would come to regret, but Jolie had wanted to take pictures of Cameron Hall so that when she returned to South Dakota she could show her family what their ancestral home looked like. The very thought of returning home and never seeing Steve again sent her into new depths of despair.

Wandering about the plantation grounds with the ever-watchful German Shepherd at her heels did little to improve her low spirits. It seemed so final to be taking pictures of the place as if she were leaving tomorrow when she had at least another week of her allotted vacation time left. She knew she would never be able to look at the pitcures once they were developed without thinking of the present owner of the plantation, of imagining him against the backdrop of flame-pink azaleas and large circular pillars.

Jolie returned to the LeBlanc home late that afternoon, arriving at the same time that Guy and Michelle did. It would have been rude to retreat to her room, although that was what she wanted to do, but Michelle had issued such a friendly invitation to join them for cold drinks that Jolie hadn't been able to refuse. Unfortunately, after only a few minutes of conversation, Michelle was called to the telephone, leaving Jolie with Guy, the one thing she had wanted to avoid.

"Cheer up, Jolie," Guy said, glancing over at her with a smile that was part amusement and part sympathy.

"What do you mean?" she asked stiffly.

"Your mouth is on the road to a permanent droop. It isn't as if you weren't warned that this would probably happen."

"I don't know what you're talking about. What would happen?" On the defensive, Jolie rose to her feet and walked over to look out the window, not seeing the red cardinal flitting about the magnolia tree.

"Claudine and Steve, of course."

"Steve's in New Orleans," Jolie said absently. Something in Guy's complacent statement made her turn around. "Isn't he?"

"You don't honestly know, do you?" Guy shook his head in amazement.

"Know what?" A terrible premonition of something bad had a grip on her chest.

"Claudine went to New Orleans with Steve."

"No!" she breathed. Her head moved from side to side in disbelief. "No, that's not true!"

A hysterical sob rose in her throat and Jolie stifled it with a clenched hand over her mouth. Now she understood the reasons for some of the things Steve had said last night. He had very tactfully been trying to tell her that he didn't care for her. He had obviously guessed the extent of her feelings and was trying to make her see that he didn't feel the same. He had even made a hint that he might use Claudine to forget Jolie, preparing her for the news that Guy had just given her.

"You really fell for him, didn't you?" Guy had come up behind her and placed his hands gently on her shoulders. She couldn't trust her voice to speak without crying so Jolie nodded agreement. "You crazy little kid," he moaned, shaking her gently before drawing her into his arms. "I told you Claudine would win."

"She didn't," Jolie answered in a shaky voice, raising her tear-filled eyes to meet his. "Don't you see? Steve doesn't care about either one of us. That's what he was trying to tell me last night."

"Last night? Did you see him last night?" Guy asked in an accusing voice.

"Yes, for a little while." Not for the world would she tell Guy how Steve had tried to frighten her away with a threatened seducement. If she had felt hurt and humiliated before, it was nothing compared to what she was suffering now. "What am I going to do, Guy?" she whispered. "I can't face him again. I just can't!"

"He had no business playing around with you," Guy declared through gritted teeth.

"It's a little late to be thinking about that now," saddened and amused by the avenging brother look on Guy's face. "Besides, it's hardly Steve's fault that I made a fool of myself," Jolie added soberly as the first wave of shock subsided. "I think maybe it's time I went home."

"To South Dakota?"

"Yes. I ran away from one problem there right into another." Determinedly she wiped her cheeks free from their tears and squared her shoulders. "If a change of scene was the cure before, it should be effective again."

"But you planned to stay another week. You told Mother you would be."

"I know what I planned," she sighed, "but... but I think it's better that I change those plans."

Jolie made the announcement to the LeBlanc family that evening at the dinner table. She used the pretext that she had received a letter from her parents, which she had, and that a close relative was ill, which wasn't true, and this had led to her sudden decision. If she packed tonight and loaded the car in the morning, she could be on the road home before Steve and Claudine returned from New Orleans.

But Jolie hadn't counted on the opposition raised by Emile LeBlanc who was insistent that she shouldn't start the long trip until her car had been checked out by a local garage. She tried desperately to assure him that this had been done thoroughly before she had left South Dakota and it was completely unnecessary for it to be done again. He was just as adamant that Jolie, who had become almost a member of his family during her short stay, should not set out on the long trip faced with the possibility of some mechanical failure of her car. Then Mrs. LeBlanc had chimed in that tomorrow was Saturday and the weekend was not a time to be driving. Finally Jolie was forced to agree to have her car checked again, but she refused to wait until Monday. She would leave Sunday morning regardless of the traffic.

By late Saturday afternoon Jolie had all her suitcases packed and ready to load into the car. Guy gave her a lift to the local garage to pick up the Volkswagen which had required only a few minor adjustments. As Jolie settled the bill, she gazed over at the young man who had become her silent supporter.

"When do you think they'll be back?" she asked quietly, knowing she didn't have to spell out that by "they" she meant Steve and Claudine.

"He probably won't drive after dark because of the fog, so they'll be home any time between now and sundown."

As it happened when Jolie and Guy returned to the LeBlanc house, it was to learn that Steve had just dropped Claudine off and had left. It was a relief to know that she wasn't going to run into him accidentally. The Fates had been kind to send her to the garage at that time to collect her car, thus saving her further embarrassment. Nor was Claudine about. She was monopolizing the bathroom after a muggy trip from New

Orleans, which made Jolie happy since she wouldn't have to suffer the older girl's smirk of triumph.

Jolie and Guy were outside arranging her suitcases in the little Volkswagen when Michelle came to the back door and told Jolie she was wanted on the telephone.

"Who is it?" Jolie asked as she glanced apprehensively at Guy.

"I didn't ask, but it sounds like Steve," Michelle answered, letting the screen door shut as she walked back into the house.

"Do you want me to tell him you're too busy to come to the phone?" Guy asked.

Jolie brushed her short hair behind her ears and breathed in deeply. "No," she said firmly, all the time wondering what kind of fool she was. "He's not likely to try to change my mind."

Her words sounded very courageous, but she felt like running as she picked up the telephone receiver lying on the table in the hallway. *Be brisk,* she told herself.

"Yes?" she said into the receiver. Her voice sounded very cool and businesslike, but her knees were trembling like jelly.

"Hello, it's Steve," he announced unnecessarily since she would have recognized his voice anywhere. "Your car was gone when I dropped Claudine off."

How could he be so offhand about it? Jolie wondered as she made a noncommittal reply. "I heard you were back from New Orleans."

"There was a football game, so the traffic was pretty heavy, or we would have been back sooner than we were."

"Look," she couldn't stand this small talk. "I'm glad you phoned. I was going to give you a ring later on," she lied, "to let you know I was leaving tomorrow to go back to South Dakota."

"What?" It was said so quietly that she almost didn't hear it.

"Yes, you see an aunt of mine is in the hospital and my folks wrote and suggested I return home. It happened rather suddenly, I guess, and she needs this operation." Why was she rattling on so as if she had to convince him of the sincerity in her reason for leaving?

"It sounds very sudden," Steve said dryly.

"Yes, well, I wanted to say goodbye before I left, which was why I was going to call you later."

"I want to talk to you, Jolie." He spoke slowly and very distinctly.

"I'm sorry. I just have so much to do before I leave—packing and so on—that it's really impossible for me to—"

"Is that Steve on the phone?"

Claudine's voice brought Jolie's hand over the receiver so the voice wouldn't carry through to Steve. Claudine was looking down at her over the stair railing dressed in a green terry cloth robe that stopped short at her knees.

"Yes, it is," Jolie answered. She asked Steve to hold the line a minute before she turned back to Claudine. "Was there something you wanted to talk to him about?"

"Yes," Claudine stated with wide eyes and a theatrical sigh as she walked the rest of the way down the steps. "I can't find my blue and green peignoir set. I've looked everywhere, but I must have inadvertently packed the nightgown in with Steve's things."

"Here." Jolie thrust the phone into Claudine's face. "You ask him."

Rigid with anger and jealousy, Jolie remembered the blue-green outfit that had reminded her of peacock feathers in all its see-through glory. Claudine shrugged at Jolie's irate gesture and calmly took the receiver.

"Steve? Claudine." She smiled sweetly at Jolie, whose feet were rooted to the floor. "You remember my blue-green gown? I can't find it and I was wondering if it had got mixed up with your things? ... It did? No ... that's not necessary. I can pick it up tomorrow ... Jolie?"

A perfectly outlined eyebrow arched questioningly at her. Jolie spun around and stalked from the hallway back outdoors.

The closed expression on Jolie's face prevented Guy from making any inquiries as she went about the packing with a vengeance. In less than a half an hour she had everything stowed in the car including the maps outlining her route. A purpling dusk was fighting off the dark of night when she locked the car door, everything in readiness for her morning's journey. Guy had gone into the house minutes before to organize refreshments.

As Jolie wiped the perspiration from her forehead, she turned toward the back door to join him. She had only taken a couple of steps when the screen door slammed shut and Jolie glanced up to see a tall figure standing in her path. Pausing, she considered fleeing, but there was nowhere to go. A grim line was drawn across her mouth as she walked toward Steve.

As she drew closer, she could see the lines of tiredness etched on his face, but she refused to allow compassion to weaken her resolve, nor her thudding heart. In the half-light, his eyes seemed an even darker blue as they watched her approach.

"You didn't have to drive all the way in," she said coolly, stopping when she was within a few feet of him.

"Didn't I?" he jeered.

"We said our goodbyes over the telephone." Pride made her chin jut out a bit more than normal.

"Our conversation was interrupted," he reminded her, unnecessarily.

"By that time everything that was important had been said. And Claudine was anxious to talk to you."

"I returned her missing gown." His gaze was flicking searchingly over her face.

"That was considerate of you. I'm sure she'll appreciate it, since she was so worried," Jolie continued to answer him calmly.

"What made you decide to leave so suddenly?"

"I already explained that my aunt is ill."

"I don't believe you. Why should the health of an aunt be of such concern to you?" he sneered.

"Aunt Brigitte is a very special person." Jolie seized the opportunity to strengthen her reasons. "She financed most of my trip down here. We've always been very close so naturally when she's ill, I just can't shrug it off as unimportant."

Her genuineness threw him. She could see the struggle in his face to disbelieve her. Here was her chance to leave, to slip away with her dignity intact.

"I have this feeling that there's something you're not saying." His quiet statement halted the beginnings of her movement.

"I don't know what it would be," Jolie swallowed, her mind racing wildly to find any loophole in her story. "I . . . I didn't thank you for showing me all the local color. It made my trip very special."

"*Lagniappe*?" A bitter questioning smile caught at her breath. Something extra, the very phrase she had first associated with him. "I had hoped to make Louisiana come alive for you."

How could she tell him that he had made her come alive? That she at last recognized the full potential of her emotions as a woman? But of course she could not. So from the depths of her agony, Jolie summoned a smile.

"You were a very romantic escort," she said, making her trembling leg muscles walk around him to stand on the first step into the house.

"Excellent for shipboard romances," he added with considerable mockery.

"Yes," she said quickly, fighting off the pain caused by the vicious thrust of his words. "It's strange how going home brings a girl's head out of the clouds."

"No embarrassing scenes. No vows of undying love. It's much better this way." There was a look of contempt in Steve's eyes that made her glad she had chosen this uncaring attitude.

"Aren't you glad now that you didn't get swept away by your emotions and do something you would live to regret?"

Steve was referring to their previous encounter the night of the fog, but Jolie could only compare it to her silence in not vocally declaring her love for him. She couldn't have stood his pity.

"Yes," she whispered, grateful the light had faded and Steve couldn't see the shimmer of tears gathering in her eyes.

"Now you'll be able to gossip with your girl friends about the man you met beside the bayou." Jolie turned her head away from the flare of his match as Steve lit a cigarette.

"It was really quite a coincidence the way you turned out to be Etienne and Etienne turned out to be Steve Cameron, the owner of Cameron Hall," she agreed in a tight voice, knowing she would never be able to tell anyone the whole story under the guise of idle gossip.

"I guess you were right when you said there wasn't any more for us to talk about. I was beginning to think I would regret the day I invited myself to your picnic." Steve sounded as if he was talking to himself, but even in the dark she could tell he was looking at her. "I guess this is goodbye, then."

A hand was extended toward her. She hesitated to take it, knowing the touch of his hand would only intensify the desire to throw herself into his arms. Her self-control didn't fail her as Jolie placed her hand in his, feeling the warmness of his firm grip spread up her arm and through her body. But it didn't ease the cold, throbbing ache in her heart that made her chest feel it was about to burst.

"Goodbye, Steve," she said softly, the words condemning her to a lifetime alone.

"'Ladybird, ladybird, fly away home,'" Steve murmured sardonically before he released her hand. "Godspeed, Jolie."

The light from inside the house made everything outside appear darker. The trees were cobwebby shapes against the first twinkling stars. Steve's form was a dark shadow before it was lost to the blackness and out of sight.

Only now could Jolie admit why the crack in her heart had not split the rest of the way. She had been hoping against hope that Steve would brush aside her weak story and masterfully sweep her into his arms telling her that he loved her too much to let her go. But, instead, he had just wished her "Godspeed."

Steve was glad to see her go. He wanted to believe her story. He felt better that she had supposedly only regarded him as a romantic escapade. That was the reality—with all the shattering results of a broken heart.

Jolie shivered. She suddenly felt so cold. So terribly cold. And alone. And empty.

CHAPTER THIRTEEN

JOLIE DIDN'T return to her parents' farm. Her destination instead was her Aunt Brigitte's apartment in Sioux Falls. After the strain of the long journey to South Dakota, during which Jolie had refused to give vent to her grief, it was natural that upon the sight of her aunt the floodgates were released and a torrent of tears burst forth.

It was the practical Brigitte Carson who took over, declaring what Jolie had been unable to, that it was impossible for her to return to her parents' home. Within a matter of only a few days Jolie had acquired a position as a dietician at a private nursing home. The salary was minimal, but money had no value to her. She needed to do something to fill in those awful, memory-filled hours.

Her aunt had been insistent that Jolie occupy the second bedroom of the apartment, at least for a while until she could get on her feet, emotionally and financially. It was just as well that Jolie had gone to her aunt since it was Brigitte who made sure she ate, got to work on time, and made the decisions that Jolie was beyond caring about.

The first week set the pattern for the following weeks. Jolie got up in the mornings, went to work, came home, ate the dinner Brigitte prepared, helped with the dishes, read a book or watched television, and went to bed.

At Christmastime Jolie made her first attempt to join in with the holiday spirits and shake off her stuporlike existence. She went to immense efforts to pick out the most appropriate and personal gift for each member of her family. The hardest one was her father, because she found that every time she walked into the men's department of a store she was visualizing what Steve would look like in a particular outfit on display. Aunt Brigitte encouraged her festive mood, indulging in buying sprees for Christmas decorations that she had considered frivolous in previous years since she had usually spent those school vacations at the farm. This year she was staying at the apartment with Jolie, who only had Christmas Day itself off work.

Several times Jolie appeared completely cheerful. Then she would exchange a look with her aunt which was always followed by a pair of silent sighs. She wasn't kidding herself or her aunt. Steve still occupied the only place in her heart.

There had been a small Christmas party at the nursing home for the patients, all of them elderly, and Jolie had volunteered to stay late and help with the cleaning up. She was feeling more depressed than usual, considering the carols of Christmastide were still ringing in her ears— probably because so many of the patients were without families or had families who conveniently forgot them. It intensified her dread of the future.

Stepping out of the nursing home, Jolie held the collar of her coat around her neck to keep out the biting cold of the north wind. Snow crunched beneath her boots while the flurries in the air promised additional inches before morning. She patted the dashboard of the Volkswagen affectionately as it started with the first turn of the switch. In weather like this, Jolie was glad her aunt's apartment was so close to where she worked.

As always, once away from the demands of her job, her thoughts strayed back to Louisiana and Steve. She had hoped, prayed, that time would lessen the vividness of her memories, but it hadn't. She had only to close her eyes and she could feel again Steve's arms around her and his kisses on her lips. And the betraying race of her pulse and the throbbing ache of her heart would laugh at her foolish wish to forget.

Parking the car in front of the ground floor apartment, Jolie firmly fixed a smile on her face before scampering into the building. It was a game she played to lift her leaden spirits. One day it might become natural and that was as far as she allowed herself to think.

"It's just me!" she called gaily, closing and locking the apartment door behind her, before removing her coat and hanging it in the hall closet. "I really think we're going to be in for a storm tonight."

She rubbed her arms briskly to give emphasis to her words as she stepped out of the small foyer into the living room. Her aunt was sitting in her favorite chair just inside the door, her brown eyes dancing mischievously up at Jolie.

"It's about time you got home," she said. "You have a visitor."

The living room stretched out to Jolie's right. Her questioning eyes followed her aunt's gaze in that direction. Steve stood near a small table holding a recently acquired Nativity scene. A white ribbed pullover sweater complemented the brown suede trousers, but Jolie's eyes were caught by the vivid blue eyes and imprisoned in their depths. The color drained from her face. He was, if it was possible, even more handsome than she remembered.

"What are you doing here?" she demanded hoarsely, unconscious of her aunt quietly slipping from the room to leave them alone.

"I came to see you," Steve answered quietly in his drawling velvet voice as he took a step toward her. There was a tenseness, a strain about his face that was more appealing than anything else.

"Get out of here! I don't want to see you!" Her hand came up to her throat to choke away the sobs that were rising.

"There are some things I've got to tell you," he continued determinedly.

"I don't want to hear them!" She turned swiftly around and would have fled to her bedroom if his hands hadn't closed over her shoulders and stopped her. It was hard to fight the desire to melt in his arms.

"I'm going to say them anyway," Steve muttered above her ear, the scent of her cologne mixing with his own masculine aroma that was intoxicating. "And after I've said them, if you still want me to leave, I will."

"Oh, please, Steve, let me go." Jolie closed her eyes tightly, hardly able to bear his nearness. "Words just don't mean anything any more."

"Not even I love you?" She was drawn back against his chest and she felt his lips moving with their caressing roughness in her hair. "I never meant to fall in love with you. Lord knows I tried not to, just as I tried to forget you. But you haunted me even before you left Louisiana. All those things I said about never marrying and not believing in love were for myself. I was a man protesting too much."

Waves of pure rapture swept over her, but she refused to give way to them. She had been through too much in these last months. There had been too many tormenting memories. Even as her heart swelled with love for him, her mind fought back.

"Even when you took Claudine to New Orleans with you?" Jolie asked.

Steve twisted her around in his arms so that he was looking into her face. "I knew you believed that's what I'd done. Maybe I even wanted to, I don't know. She called me and asked to ride along, but I swear to you, we stayed in separate hotels. And that damned gown she was talking about was an evening gown she picked up at the dry-cleaners the day we left New Orleans. She left it in the car."

"Why didn't you tell me that?" Jolie whispered. Some of the fight went out of her as she gazed into the face she adored.

"You were so ready to believe the worst," he smiled ruefully, deepening the grooves near his mouth. "And so ready to have me believe that

I was just a passing fancy to you. A shipboard romance.''

"You were never that," Jolie admitted shyly.

"Are you sure, Jolie, very sure?" Steve demanded, the fierceness coming back into his eyes. "Because these last few months without you have been hell."

Her arms slid around his neck and pulled his head closer to hers. It was like coming home after a very long time. The need for words had come to an end as Steve took over her initial movement for his kiss, changing it into a hungry embrace that left her in no doubt as to the depth of his feelings. She was quite sure her response was equally revealing.

Much later, they had somehow traversed to the small sofa and Jolie was cradled in his lap where he could kiss and caress her at will. His will was strong and Jolie was willing.

"Do I give you a few minutes or just walk in?" Aunt Brigitte called from just outside the living room door.

Jolie started to struggle upright, but Steve held her in place. "Come on in," Steve directed, smiling mischievously at Jolie's flushed cheeks. "Your niece is behaving very wantonly. I think she's in grave need of a chaperon."

"A maid of honor might be more appropriate," Aunt Brigitte commented dryly at the sight of the pair, but with a decided twinkle of happiness and approval in her understanding brown eyes.

"It's something you'd better be thinking about, little Miss Ladybird," said Steve, planting a firm kiss on her lips as he pushed Jolie onto the sofa beside him. "Because whether I've asked you or not, we're going to be married just as soon as we can get a licence and a minister. Cameron Hall is in need of another Jolie Antoinette Cameron as mistress, and so is the master."

"That was a proposal in front of a witness, Mr. Cameron," Jolie gazed adoringly into his face. "And in front of a witness, I accept."

"I don't think Steve intended to give you much of a choice," her aunt smiled. "I don't have any champagne for the celebration, but I could make some cocoa."

"Do you want some help?" Jolie offered, disliking the thought of leaving Steve's side even for a moment. She needn't have worried, because her offer was firmly refused.

"Before I forget," said Steve, addressing himself to her aunt as he put an arm around Jolie and drew her closer to him, "Jolie told me that you were responsible for her being able to take that trip to Louisiana. I want to thank you for that, from both of us. If Jolie has no objections, I thought we might name our first girl after you."

The older woman's eyes became starry bright with tears as she smiled and said, "Only if I can be her godmother."

"Consider it done," Jolie stated, feeling the same tightness in her throat that had been in her aunt's.

"Well, I'd better make that cocoa." And her aunt hastily left the room.

"Did you mind?" Steve asked, gazing down at her with unbelievable warmth.

"I thought it was wonderful." A shy blush covered her cheeks. "We could have boys, though."

"We'll just have to keep trying until we get it right," he teased, laughing at her open-mouthed expression. "Darling, at the moment I don't care if we have two, ten, or twenty children. All I want is you. Anything else will be a bonus, although a boy and a girl would be nice."

"Oh, Steve, I love you so much," she said breathlessly, gazing into the face that she had been so afraid she would never see again.

It was an invitation he couldn't resist. And neither could Jolie as she offered her lips to his.

"And I love you," he whispered against her mouth.

... And now an exciting preview of

SWEET PROMISE
another Janet Dailey title
coming in October

Erica was starved for love. Daughter of a Texas millionaire who had time only for business, she'd thought up a desperate scheme to get her father's attention.

Unfortunately her plan backfired and she found herself seriously involved with Rafael de la Torres, a man she believed to be a worthless fortune hunter.

That had been a year ago; the affair had almost ruined her life. Now she was in love with a wonderful man. But she wasn't free to marry him. First of all she must find Rafael...!

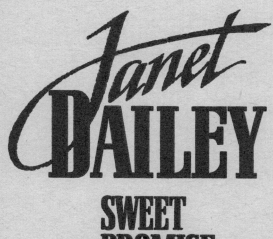

SWEET PROMISE

CHAPTER ONE

THE MUSIC was a slow, sentimental ballad, spinning its love theme for the few couples on the floor. The subdued lighting added to the magic of the moment, creating another romantic spell.

A happy sigh slid through Erica's lips as she felt the caressing touch of Forest's chin against her dark hair. Her fingers curled tighter around his neck while she lightly rubbed the side of her head along his chin and jawline in a feline gesture, smiling when she felt his mouth against her hair.

Tilting her head back she gazed into his tanned face, admiring again his striking looks; the commanding strength in repose signified by the square jaw and the cleft in his chin, the sensual line of his mouth, and the velvet touch of his brown eyes as they possessively examined her face.

To speak in a normal voice might break the spell, so Erica whispered softly instead. "Would it sound very corny and silly if I said that I could do this all night?"

"With me or with anyone?" Forest murmured. An eyebrow, the same light brown shade as his hair, arched to tease her.

"That's another thing I like about you. You never take me for granted." Her soft voice trembled with the depth of her emotion and Erica buried her head in his shoulder, knowing her violet eyes were much too expressive of her thoughts.

"What else do you like about me?" His lips were moving against the silken length of her hair again, igniting warm fires in her veins.

"Conceited?" she taunted him, but with a catch in her husky voice.

"Where you are concerned I need all the assurance I can get." The arm around her waist tightened, holding her closer to his muscular body as if he expected her to slip away. "Tell me." His growling order was a mock threat, but one Erica was only too happy to obey.

Hesitant to reveal how deeply she cared for this man who was noted for his careless and carefree association with women, she adopted a light-hearted air.

"For starters, you don't make all those affirmative noises when daddy is around. You're independent and very secure about your own ability. You're much too handsome for a girl's peace of mind. Elusive, always managing to escape being led down to the altar and all the while making a girl believe she's the only one in your life.'' Erica raised her head from his shoulder and encountered the smoldering light in his eyes. With her lashes, she shielded the answering light in her own eyes. "A girl wants to forget everything her parents taught her when she's with you.''

"Not all girls.'' His hand cupped her chin, lifting it so he could gaze thoughtfully into her face. "Certainly not you. That first night I took you out, I was ready to agree that all those rumors about your being an ice maiden were true. To be perfectly honest, Erica, in the beginning you were a challenge.'' White teeth flashed as his mouth curved in a rueful smile. "I don't believe anyone has said no to me as many times as you have.''

Determinedly she forced herself to breathe evenly. "Do you mean all those times you invited me to your apartment, it wasn't to see your art collection?'' she teased, her eyes widening with false surprise.

"Only the one in my bedroom.'' The laughter left his face as he studied her solemnly. "Every time I touch you or kiss you, I sense that you're holding back. I know you're Vance Wakefield's daughter and many men have taken you out not only because of your looks but because of his wealth and influence. Surely you know me well enough by now to realize that I'm not the least bit interested in who your father is."

"I know that." Their steps had nearly ceased as they absently swayed in tempo with the music.

"Not that I haven't taken into account that you're his daughter to the extent that he is your father and very important in your life," Forest added. "That's the way it should be, even though I know he doesn't totally approve of me."

"It's not you he disapproves of, but your reputation." Erica shrugged weakly.

"And that I may in some way sully yours." He nodded understandingly.

"Daddy isn't an ogre," she said, smiling humorlessly. "He sees me as an adult and realizes that my relationships with other people are on an adult level."

There was no need to add that if Vance Wakefield felt his daughter was being used, he would fall upon the offender with all the weight his power and money could bring to bear. Yet that was not a comforting thought for Erica. In the almost twenty-two years of her life, she had tried very hard to become close to her father. He was a strong, indomitable, ruthless man who despised weakness of any sort. She seriously doubted if he had ever mourned the loss of his wife, her mother, but rather cursed her inability to survive the birth of a child, Erica.

In her early years she had fought for his love, always terrified that her handsome father would marry again and she would have to compete with a new wife and possibly another child for the attention she wanted so desperately. No other woman entered his household, but he became married to his business, a more jealous and demanding rival than Erica could compete against and win. Still she fought and struggled for every ounce of attention that she could steal, using every weapon from open rebellion and stormy scenes to smothering love.

It had taken her nearly twenty years to realize that in his own way he loved her. As strong as the bonds were, she was still a female, hence weak. And Erica concealed any exploit that would point out her vulnerability and lower his esteem of her.

"If it's not your father's wrath you fear, why have you refused me?" A frown of puzzlement drew Forest's brows together. "You aren't an ice maiden—I've discovered that. There have been times when I've held you in my arms that I've been certain I touched a core of passion inside you. Don't you want me as much as I want you? Or don't you trust me?"

"Oh, no, I don't trust myself," she corrected quickly. She could feel the glowing heat of previous shame rising in her cheeks and murmured a silent prayer of thanks for the dimness of the room that concealed it.

"And you've been afraid to do something in the heat of the moment that you would regret in the cold light of day," he finished for her, a gentle and satisfied smile curving the strong line of his mouth.

"Yes, that's what I have been afraid of," Erica admitted. It was a fear that had very firm foundation.

The last note of the song was tapering into silence. For a second, Forest retained his hold, keeping her pressed against his long length, and Erica wondered if he had caught the qualifying statement she had just made. She had been afraid, but she wasn't any longer.

Two months wasn't a very long time in which to know a man. Still, Erica was positive that what she felt toward Forest was not simply physical attraction or even sexual attraction, but a deeper emotion called love, however futile it might be.

A musician in the small combo announced they would be taking a short break and all the couples had left the dance floor by the time Forest guided Erica back to their table. His arm retained a possessive hold on her waist, relinquishing it only when they were seated, their chairs drawn closely together.

"I'm beginning to understand more things about you," Forest said softly, letting his arm curve over the back of her chair to caress her bare shoulders. "But I've been making even stranger discoveries about myself."

"About you? Such as?" prompted Erica, tucking a strand of shoulder-length dark hair behind her ear so it wouldn't interfere with her view of him.

"Such as—" His gaze wandered over her face, lingering on her lips "—I've fallen in love with you, irrevocably and irretrievably in love with you."

Her gasp was a mixture of disbelief and elation. She had never dared hope that he might care as much as she believed she did. The wonder of it darkened her eyes to a royal shade of purple heightened by a diamond mist of happy tears.

"I love you, too," Erica breathed. "I never believed...I never thought it was possible that you might love me."

"Only a man in love would take no for an answer as many times as I have." He smiled, and something in his smile confirmed the truth of his words.

She wanted to wind her arms around his neck and feel the warmth of his lips against hers, but just then laughter sounded from one of the tables near theirs and Erica was reminded that they were not alone.

"If you doubted my feelings," Forest murmured, his hand intimately caressing the curve of her neck, "can you imagine how I wondered about yours? I felt you were bound to mistrust me because of my reputation. I've heard some of the stories that have been circulated about me, and some were based on fact."

"It's never mattered to me what others have said about you," she insisted.

She wanted to explain that one of the things that had drawn her to him was his somewhat diehard bachelor attitude, but to do that would mean explaining her reasons and she hadn't the courage for that yet.

"Shall we drink a toast then, to each other?" he suggested. His fingers closed around the stem of his martini glass and Erica reached for her own glass. Compared to his strong drink, hers was an innocuous sherry. Over their glasses their eyes met, sending silent messages while the expensive crystal rang when their glasses touched.

"I think there's something in my martini," Forest declared, drawing the glass near the light after the first tentative sip to study it.

"Besides the olive?" Her tremulous smile was to cover the fluttering of her heart as she covertly studied his profile.

"Would you look at this?" His voice was amused and vaguely triumphant as he directed her gaze to the miniature plastic spear in his hand.

At the end of the spear was the olive with its stuffing of red pimento, but dangling in front of it was a ring. The muted candlelight touched the stone and reflected myriad colors.

"This must be yours." At his announcement, Erica swung her stunned look to him.

"No." Her head moved to deny it.

He had wiped it dry with his linen handkerchief and was now handing the ring to her. "I hope you're going to accept it," he said. "It might be poetic justice to have the first girl I've ever proposed to turn me down. But after all this time of saying no, now that I'm asking you to marry me, please say yes, darling."

Somehow she eluded his move to place the ring on her finger, taking it instead and clutching it between the fingers of both hands. The single diamond solitaire winked back at her, laughing at her until her head throbbed with pain as Erica fought to stem the hysteria that bubbled in her throat.

"Don't you like it?" His voice was low and controlled, but with a razor-sharp edge to it.

The face she turned to him was unnaturally pale and strained. "Oh, Forest, I love it," she gulped, tearing her gaze from the mocking ring to meet his, only to bounce back to the diamond when she was unable to meet the probing brown eyes. A tear slipped from her lashes to blaze a hot trail down her cheek, but she quickly wiped it away. "Please—may we leave here?"

"Of course."

Erica knew Forest would misinterpret her reasons for wanting to go, believing that she wanted a less public place for her tears of happiness. They were tears of happiness. The salty tang of them on her lips was what brought the bitterness and produced the misery of the moment.

With the ease of a man who knew his way about, Forest disposed of their check, produced the light shawl that matched the layered chiffon dress she wore, and had the car brought around to the front of the club.

Moments later he had turned the car onto a quiet San Antonio street and was switching off the engine. Not one word had he directed to her, and he didn't now as he drew her into his arms. Her lips hungrily sought his descending mouth, welcoming and returning the ardency of his touch while his hands arched her toward him. Her unbridled response unnerved both of them and it took some minutes before they were able to recover their powers of speech.

Forest's mouth was moving over her eyes and cheeks. "Will you marry me, darling?" His breath caressed her skin as he spoke. "Or do I have to carry you off into the night until you agree?"

"I want to marry you," Erica whispered, a throbbing ache in her voice. "More than anything else, I want you to believe that."

For all her fervid assurance, his searching kiss stopped, halted by the unspoken qualification in her statement. His tensed stiffness tore at her chest. The ring was still in her hand, burning its imprint in her sensitive palm.

"But I can't accept your ring." She added the words Forest had instinctively braced himself to hear.

"Why?" The demand was combined with the tightening of his hold just before he thrust her away. "You do love me?"

"I love you, darling, honestly I do," vowed Erica, caressing the tanned cheek with her hand. "I simply can't accept your ring. At least not now, I can't."

There was a slightly imperious and bemused tilt of his head. "I've always known you were old-fashioned in some ways, but I never guessed that you would want me to speak to your father first."

"No, that's not what I meant!" Her cry was one of despair and panic.

"I don't understand," Forest sighed impatiently, wearily rubbing the back of his neck. "Do you want to marry me or not?"

"Yes, I want to—oh, please, Forest, I can't take your ring. It wouldn't be fair." She begged for his understanding, to have the touch of his hands become once more loving.

"Are you engaged to someone else?" An incredulous anger narrowed his gaze.

"No!" She pressed her fingers against the pounding pain between her eyes. "I can't explain and I beg you not to ask me. I swear it's true that I love you, but I need time."

He stared at her for a long moment, his expression carved and impenetrable before a slow smile broke the severe mold. "It is a big step, isn't it? I've had plenty of time to think it over, but I haven't given you much warning."

Time for a decision was not what Erica had meant, but she was very willing to take advantage of it. She opened her clenched hand and stared at the ring. The starlight streaming through the car windows cast a milky sheen on the many facets of the large diamond.

"It is a big step," she agreed, taking a deep breath. "Not something that's done on the spur of the moment." The only smile she could summon was somewhat twisted and wry, its ruefulness concealed by the dimness. "Marry in haste, repent at leisure. I don't want it to be that way with us, Forest.''

"Neither do I. I want you to be as certain as I am," he stated.

Although she didn't look up, she could feel the caress of his eyes. The calm determination of his voice almost made her want to put the ring on her finger and damn the consequences, but she steeled herself against doing anything so foolish. Slowly she stretched out her hand to him, palm upward, the engagement ring in the center.

"Would you keep this for me?" she asked. As she met the controlled desire in his gaze, the pain at giving back his ring softened and she sought to reassure him. "I think I'll be wanting it shortly, so please don't give it to some other girl."

"I burned all my telephone numbers weeks ago. There is no other girl." His light brown hair gleamed golden in the pale light as he bent his head to retrieve his ring.

When the ring was safely in his pocket, his velvet brown eyes skittered over her face, its oval perfection framed by the rich brown hair combed away from it. His searching glance came to a full stop on the curve of her lips.

"Don't make me wait too long, Erica." It wasn't a request because of the autocratic ring of his voice. Nor was it a threat, since passion throbbed beneath the surface.

"I won't." The starlight gilded her smooth complexion as she waited in anticipation of the moment when Forest would draw her firmly in his arms.

His hand trailed lightly over the hollow of her cheek back to the base of her neck, sliding under her hair as a thumb gently rubbed the pulsing vein in her neck.

"No woman has ever dangled me on a string before," he told her, his expression paradoxically tender and hard. "I don't like it." Erica started to initiate the movement that would bring her to the muscular chest, but his hand tightened around her neck to check it. Then he released her and turned to the front. "I'm taking you home. I haven't much patience left, so the sooner you make the decision, the better off I will be."

Erica was given no opportunity to argue as he started the car and drove it back onto the street. Part of her wanted the evening to last forever, not to go on torturing Forest as her lack of an answer was doing, but to postpone what she was going to be forced to do if she wanted to marry him. And Erica was certain that she did.

The closer they came to her home on the outskirts of the city, the more her thoughts became preoccupied with her dilemma. When Forest walked her to the door, the kiss she gave him appeared natural enough on the surface, but underneath her nerves were becoming raw from the strain of her decision.

When she stepped inside the house, she discovered her legs were trembling. Their weakness had no basis in Forest's ardent kiss. Her widened eyes, like fully opened African violets, darted to the closed study door, almost the only room in the large, rambling house that her father used. In her mind's eye, Erica could visualize the freezing scorn and contempt that would pierce the blue depths of his eyes if she went to him with her problem.

It had never been his contempt that she had feared. There had been times in the past when she had deliberately provoked his wrath to gain his attention. Only once had her actions backfired on her, the very last time she had done it. Only afterward had she realized how very foolish her childish attempts had been.

But it had succeeded in forcing her to grow up. And Erica had finally realized that her father was incapable of loving her as much as she loved him. In many ways their temperaments were alike. She could be as bullheaded and stubborn as he and just as quick to anger. Yet Vance Wakefield was not able to give of himself and he had never been able to understand her need as a child to be constantly assured of his affection.

Her coming of age had opened her eyes to this one flaw of her father's. In the past almost two years, Erica had stopped demanding more than he could give. Their relationship had reached a peak of casual companionship that she had never thought they could attain. To go to him now would destroy it.

Her teeth sank sharply into her lower lip to bite back the sob of despair. Casting a last furtive glance at the study, she hurried down the hallway to her bedroom. When the oak door was closed behind her, she leaned weakly against it, then pushed herself away to cross the Persian carpet of a richly patterned blue and gold. Her fingers closed tightly around the carved oak bedpost while her darkly clouded eyes stared at the brilliant sea of blue of the bedspread.

Her first impulse was to throw herself on the bed, to wallow in a pool of self-pity that she was ever foolish enough to get into such a situation. Instead Erica shook her head determinedly, banishing the impulse as a waste of energy. She tipped her head back and stared at the ceiling, breathing in deeply to calm her jumping nerves. Low, mocking laughter surged through the tight muscles of her throat, its echo taunting her as it sounded through the room.

"I've spent nearly two years hiding and dreading this day," she chided herself. "I kept stupidly believing that it would all work out on its own."

She buried her head in her hands, refusing to cry as she forced her mind to search for a solution—any solution that would not involve going to her father. Lifting her head out of her hands and letting her fingers close over her throat, she sighed dispiritedly. If only she had someone to talk to, she thought dejectedly. Someone close who would understand what had prompted her to do such a stupid thing. She refused to take the chance of confiding in Forest and risk the loss of his love.

She had no close girl friends, at least, none she would trust with this kind of damaging information. As she was growing up, her father had insisted she attend private schools, snobbishly believing they offered a better and broader education. At the same time Erica had thought he was sending her to these expensive boarding schools because he didn't care about her. Only now could she see that he simply had not known what to do with a young child under his roof. The few friends she had made lived in other parts of the country and after more than four years of separation, correspondence between them had ceased except for annual Christmas cards.

Lawrence Darby, her father's secretary and Man Friday, had always been a sympathetic sounding board in the past, but Erica was totally aware that he automatically carried any major problem to Vance Wakefield, the very thing she wanted to avoid. Not that Lawrence would deliberately betray her; he would only be turning to the man he knew would have the connections and influence to solve her problem.

As for relatives, Erica only had aunts and uncles and cousins, none of whom were overly concerned about her personal problems or even whether she had any. She drew a sharp breath of hope.

"Uncle Jules," she murmured. "Oh, how stupid! Why didn't I think of him before?"

Jules Blackwell was not related to her at all, but he had grown up with Vance Wakefield and was one of her father's rare friends. When Erica was born, Jules Blackwell had appointed himself as her godparent and had taken an active interest in her life. His affection she had never doubted, in fact took for granted. His position and profession were independent of her father's and therefore Jules looked on her father as a man and not the powerful Vance Wakefield. And the man she had affectionately titled "uncle" was aware of the struggle she had made to win her father's love. He could be trusted not to race to her father.

Equally important as all the other reasons was the knowledge that Jules Blackwell was an attorney of some renown. For the first time in nearly two years, the yoke of shame and guilt seemed to ease its ponderous weight from her shoulders and Erica wanted to cry with relief. But the time for weeping was when success was in her grasp.

Dashing to the polished oak chest of drawers, she rummaged through the expensive lingerie until her fingers closed around the knotted handkerchief buried in one corner. Hot color raged over her skin at the touch of the heavy metal object penetrating the material. The red stain didn't leave her cheeks until the knotted handkerchief was buried again, this time in the bottom of her purse.

Sleep eluded her so that most of her rest came in fitful dozes. Still Erica tarried in bed as long as she could the next morning to avoid meeting her father. When she arrived in the sunny yellow breakfast room, only Lawrence was still seated.

"You're late this morning." He smiled, his eyes crinkling behind wire-rimmed glasses. He was only two years older than Forest, yet his receding hairline and thinness added at least ten years.

"I overslept," Erica fibbed, helping herself to toast and marmalade before pouring a cup of coffee for herself.

"Vance has already eaten, but he asked me to pass a message on to you."

"What's that?" Subconsciously she was holding her breath as she took a chair opposite Lawrence.

"The first part was to remind you about the dinner tonight at the Mendelsens' and the second was to suggest that you invite Mr. Granger to accompany you."

Her surprised glance took in the rather smug expression. Her father's suggestions were virtually royal commands, and never before had he even hinted one of her dates should be included in an invitation extended to them.

"Did you have any part in his suggestion, Lawrence?" A knowing smile played with the corners of her mouth.

"No one makes decisions for your father." But there was a twinkle in the pale blue eyes that indicated he had undoubtedly introduced Forest's name into the conversation. "I think Vance is beginning to realize there might be something serious developing between you two."

It was a probing remark designed to inspire confidence, but Erica knew her reply would be passed on to her father. It was his indirect way of remaining involved in her life without taking the time to inquire for himself.

"It's a bit soon to be certain, but it could be serious." It was serious, but Erica didn't want to admit that until she had her other problem solved. "I'll call Forest when I get to the boutique and find out if he's free this evening."

"How is business?" Lawrence inquired.

"I believe daddy is going to be very surprised when he receives my monthly report," she declared, raising a complacent brow as she sipped her coffee.

More than a year ago Erica had persuaded her father that she needed an outside interest, some reason for getting up in the morning. It was beneath his dignity to allow her to be employed by someone. She was Vance Wakefield's daughter. Erica doubted that her father had actually believed she was serious. To humor her, he had financed the setting up of a small boutique along the landscaped riverwalk.

Along with some of his other traits, Erica had also inherited his business acumen. At the end of her first year in business, the exclusive dress shop had broken even. Now, partly due to nearly flawless taste in fashions and her keen management, it was beginning to show a profit. Being responsible for its success or failure had also made Erica appreciate more the endless demands her father's multiple interests placed upon him.

The instant Lawrence left the breakfast nook, all conscious thought of the boutique vanished. The haste that made Erica leave her toast and coffee half-finished was due to a desire to arrive at the shop and call Jules Blackwell in privacy where there was no risk that her father or Lawrence could accidentally overhear.

The boutique, appropriately called Erica, was already open when Erica arrived. As she locked the doors of her sports car, she said a silent prayer of thanks that she had acquired a clerk as trustworthy and conscientious as Donna Kemper, a petite attractive blonde in her early thirties, divorced and with two little school-age girls. With Donna and a teenage girl named Mary who helped part-time after school, Erica had discovered the shop could survive without her constant supervision.

There was only one customer in the store when she walked in. Smiling a hello to the woman, Erica murmured a friendly greeting to Donna.

"The shipment has arrived from Logan's," Donna informed her.

Erica's head bobbed in wry acknowledgment. "I have some calls to make, then I'll be out to give you a hand."

A wide smile of understanding spread across the fair woman's face. "We've waited this long to receive it. Another few hours before it's on the rack won't make much difference."

Then the customer required Donna's attention and Erica walked to the back of the store to the small alcove hidden in the storage section. After she dialed Jules's office number, she sifted through the mail Donna had placed on the desk, schooling her hammering heart to slow down. It was several minutes before his secretary was able to connect her with Jules. He was plainly delighted and surprised that she had called. The open affection in his voice made her wish she had done it earlier and not have to seek him out now when she had a problem.

"I was calling to see if you would be free around lunchtime, Uncle Jules." Erica explained in answer to his question.

"Are you asking me out to lunch, young lady?" His teasing laughter lifted her spirits. "Because if you are, I'm accepting."

"Actually, I am," she smiled at the beige-colored receiver, visualizing the rotund, ever smiling face on the opposite end.

"Good. Where would you like me to meet you?"

Erica hesitated. "I...I was hoping I could see you for a few minutes at your office."

Her statement was followed by a small silence before he spoke again, the laughter giving way to solemnness. "Are you and Vance having problems again?"

"No, not exactly," she hedged.

He must have sensed her unwillingness to discuss it over the telephone. "All right. I'll expect you here at eleven-thirty. How's that?"

"Thank you." She sighed.

"Don't worry. Uncle Jules will fix it, whatever it is."

When Erica replaced the receiver, a tentative smile was gleaming in her eyes. With her burden lightened, she telephoned Forest, who very willingly accepted the invitation her father had extended.

Harlequin American Romance

Romances that go one step farther...
American Romance

Realistic stories involving people you can relate to and care about.

Compelling relationships between the mature men and women of today's world.

Romances that capture the core of genuine emotions between a man and a woman.

Join us each month for four new titles wherever paperback books are sold.
Enter the world of American Romance.

Amro-1

Harlequin Romance

Enter the world of Romance...
Harlequin Romance

Delight in the exotic yet innocent love stories of
Harlequin Romance.

Be whisked away to dazzling international capitals... or
quaint European villages.

Experience the joys of falling in love... for the first
time, the best time!

Six new titles every month for your reading enjoyment.
Available wherever paperbacks are sold.

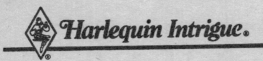

Harlequin Intrigue

They went in through the terrace door. The house was dark, most of the servants were down at the circus, and only Nelbert's hired security guards were in sight. It was child's play for Blackheart to move past them, the work of two seconds to go through the solid lock on the terrace door. And then they were creeping through the darkened house, up the long curving stairs, Ferris fully as noiseless as the more experienced Blackheart.

They stopped on the second floor landing. "What if they have guns?" Ferris mouthed silently.

Blackheart shrugged. "Then duck."

"How reassuring," she responded. Footsteps directly above them signaled that the thieves were on the move, and so should they be.

For more romance, suspense and adventure, read Harlequin Intrigue. Two exciting titles each month, available wherever Harlequin Books are sold.

INTA-1